Phone power

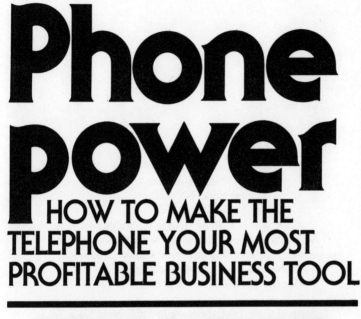

Phone power

HOW TO MAKE THE TELEPHONE YOUR MOST PROFITABLE BUSINESS TOOL

GEORGE R. WALTHER

G. P. Putnam's Sons
New York

G. P. Putnam's Sons
Publishers Since 1838
200 Madison Avenue
New York, NY 10016

Library of Congress Cataloging-in-Publication Data

Walther, George R.
Phone power.

Bibliography: p.
Includes index.
1. Telephone in business.   I. Title.
HE8735.W34   1986   658.4′52   85-28225
ISBN 0-399-13137-X

Printed in the United States of America
2   3   4   5   6   7   8   9   10

ACKNOWLEDGMENTS

The term "Phone Power" may have a familiar ring to you. Perhaps you remember the Bell System pamphlets and seminars of the same name publicized during the 1960s. This book is neither associated with, nor the result of, those materials, though its mission is similar. My hat is off to the Bell System pioneers who helped motivate and train businesspeople to get more results when using their phones.

This book didn't come out of my head. It's the result of techniques practiced every day by the true phone pros—those whose intuitive good sense and courtesy leads them to treat me—and you—well in every conversation. They don't put us on interminable hold, they don't transfer us endlessly, they don't wander aimlessly, and they don't say "That's not my job."

Thousands have attended my telephone seminars expecting only to learn. But they ended up teaching, too. I thank them for their valuable suggestions, questions and concerns.

The idea for this book was born in the same week that I met Julie. She was instrumental in shaping the manuscript. I'm blessed with a happy marriage and a book I'm proud of. Without her, I would have neither.

Rosemarie Chatman tirelessly and cheerfully revised this manuscript repeatedly without complaint. I thank her for the many times she said, "No problem, I'll just stay till it's finished."

My fine agents, Arthur and Richard Pine, have made it possible for me to concentrate on the book and leave the business to them. I thank them for the many doors they continue opening for me.

You've probably heard the sad tales of frustrated authors tromping from publisher to publisher only to receive rejection slips. Mine was different. A savvy editor, Adrienne Ingrum, sensed a need for all of us to unleash the power locked up in our taken-for-granted telephones. She nurtured me with helpful ideas, encouraged me over the hard parts, and freed me from all the usual authors' complaints.

To Julie, my partner, my love, and my bride.

To Julie, my partner, my love, and my best...

CONTENTS

PREFACE

Phone Power is no business theory book: it's filled with practical techniques and strategies that can help every businessperson, in any position, unleash the profit power of the telephone.

Phone Power is focused on the principles of "conscious contact." Major time savings and leveraged profit gains result from your conscious application of simple contact strategies.

Many of the conscious contact techniques, such as ways to avoid playing phone tag, or how to project positive impressions with your voice, apply to everyone who uses a phone. But others concern "goal phoning," calling with the intent of achieving a specific objective. If your goal is to upgrade an organization's public image, you may turn immediately to chapter 4, "Phone Relations." When you're about to call an unhappy customer, be sure to review chapter 6, "Wired Emotions." The next time your goal is to conclude a successful negotiation, turn to chapter 7, "Phonegotiating." Use this book as a reference guide in your business library.

Phone Power will also give you a glimpse of future phone technology and will recommend a few gadgets. But this isn't a book about hardware.

Don't keep *Phone Power* a secret. Be sure your secretary reads chapter 3 so you can establish an effective call-screening system together. Every switchboard operator and receptionist should see chapter 5. And your Customer Service staff will be glad they read chapter 6 next time an irate caller starts shouting. The Accounts Receivable manager can dramatically improve your profit picture by studying chapter 8.

Every person in your organization is within an arm's reach of the most profitable power tool in business. Be sure they all tap its full potential. This book delivers exactly what its title promises: *Phone Power: How to Make the Telephone Your Most Profitable Business Tool.*

INTRODUCTION: YOUR MOST UNDERVALUED BUSINESS ALLY

Receptionist: *[Bored, nasal]* "Four-oh-six, twelve hundred, hold please." *[More than a minute later . . .]* "Who are you calling for?"

Caller: "Ms. Esther, please."

Receptionist: "Your name?"

Caller: "George Walther. That's W-A-L-T-H-E-R."

Receptionist: "What company?"

Caller: "TelExcel. I'll spell that for you: T-E-L, E-X-C-E-L—"

Receptionist: "Hold, please." *[One minute and fifteen seconds later, the receptionist returns to the line. Other voices are chattering in the background.]* "Marsha Esther is all tied up right now; I'll take your number."

Caller: "Yes, please do. It's 2-1-3, 8-2—" *[A third voice interrupts.]*

Third voice: "Hello?"

Receptionist: "Oh, Marsha, this is Mr. Wolper from Trexel. It's for you."

Third voice: "Hello Mr. Wolper. What can I do for ya?"

Caller: "Good morning, Ms. Esther, I understand that you handle Mr. Gilchrest's calendar. He and I have been having a hard time connec—" *[Nasal voice interrupts.]*

Receptionist: "Four-oh-six, twelve hundred—"

Third voice: "It's okay, Susan; I've got it! Now, Mr. Wolper. I don't exactly know when you can reach Mr. Gilchrest. I'll have to check and call you back."

Caller: "That's fine. I'm also quite busy, so let's agree on a time and I'll be sure to wait for your call. Is eleven-thirty, your time, convenient?"

Third voice: "Yes, I'll call you at eleven-thirty."

Caller: "Good. My direct private number is 213-555-4100."

Third voice: "Okay, then. I'll be—" *[Nasal voice interrupts.]*

Receptionist: "Four-oh-six, twelve hundred—"

Third voice: "I've got it, Susan. Now, uh . . ."

Next day, the cycle began all over again. Ms. Esther never called. The irony of this particular call is that Marsha Esther is a high-ranking executive in a very well-known telemarketing consulting firm. Although you'd expect a telephone firm to use impeccable telephone techniques, this episode actually occurred. It was one of the worst I've experienced.

Does it sound painfully similar to calls you have placed?

James first calls Roger about the tickets at 9:15 A.M. Roger's running late this morning, so James leaves a message. At 9:46, when Roger returns the call, James is in a staff meeting. His secretary takes the message. When the session finally breaks, James calls Roger and finds that he's lunching with a client at La Crêperie. At 2:30 Roger's back, but now James is out with a client for the afternoon.

The next morning, they connect. "I wish we'd made contact yesterday, Roger, I had two extra seats for last night's World Series playoff."

How many times did you play "phone tag" last week? How many times were you "It"?

Customer: "Hello. Listen, I want to speak with you because no one else at your company seems to be able to help me. I don't know why your people can't get their acts together. I've gotten the wrong compressor belt sent to me repeatedly. What do I have to do to get things straightened out?"

Vice President: "I'm sorry about that, sir. Have you been in contact with the customer service department?"

Customer: "Of *course* I have. They just give me the

runaround! They put me on hold and then cut me off. Why can't I get a simple order corrected without so much hassle?"

Vice President: "There's no need to get so upset, sir. Customer Service should be able to try to get it fixed up right away."

Customer: *[Louder]* "Let me tell you something. I've just about had it with your company! I've been buying from you for years, and things are just getting worse and worse. I don't have time to get bogged down—" *[Click. Silence.]*

Had one of those calls lately? You know the customer was out of line. But was he right? Did you and your people help the situation or make it worse? Will that customer ever buy from you again? And to how many of his friends will he bad-mouth your company?

Julie: "Hello. I'm calling because I just got turned down for a car loan, and the dealer said that my credit report shows a delinquent Visa record."

First Clerk: "Oh, you want the credit department. Hang on." *[One minute and forty-six seconds later . . .]*

Second Clerk: "Credit, please hold." *[A few seconds later]* "Yes?"

Julie: "Hello. I want to find out why my credit report shows a delinquent Visa record. I've been paying on time every month for three—"

Second Clerk: "You'll have to talk to the main office. The number is 818-555-7679."

Julie: "But that's long-distance. Isn't there some way you can help me? You're my branch."

Second Clerk: "Sorry, you'll have to call Pasadena." *[Julie calls headquarters.]*

Julie: "Hello. I'm calling because I just got turned down for a car loan, and the dealer said that my credit report shows a delinquent Visa record."

Third Clerk: "Just a minute, I'll get the credit department for you."

Fourth Clerk: "Processing, this is Judy. I'll be right with you." *[Six minutes pass. The music-on-hold is a bit too loud and Julie really doesn't feel like hearing "Rock Me, Baby"!]* "Hello, can I help you?"

Julie: "I sure hope so. I've been transferred all over. My Visa record has a mistake. I pay at my branch every month, and —."

Fourth Clerk: "David handles all payment records. He's at lunch, but I'll give him the message."

Julie: "Please tell him to call me this afternoon at 213-555-1327. This afternoon, for sure, okay?"

Fourth Clerk: "Sure." *[Julie waits, but no call. Next morning.]*

Julie: "David was supposed to call me yesterday because there's a mistake on my credit record."

Fifth Clerk: "David's in a meeting right now. Can you call back after lunch?"

Julie: "*Again?* I keep calling you long-distance and I just want to get my Visa records straight. I have all the payment receipts from my branch."

Fifth Clerk: "Oh, if you make your payments locally, you really should be calling the branch directly."

Julie: "But they told me to call you!"

Fifth Clerk: "Oh. Well, maybe you should call whatever credit agency reported the account as delinquent."

Julie: "I have! They said to call my bank!"

My wife finally resolved the problem. It took several more phone calls, and ultimately required a person-to-person conversation with a senior bank officer.

Isn't that about how things went when you last called your bank? How about when you called the Post Office, or the IRS, or your utility company?

Accounts Receivable (A/R) Agent: "Hello, Mr. Perlman. This is James McQuaily at Jiffy Instant Printers. I'm calling again because your account is more than ninety days past due and you did promise to send in your payment a month and a half ago."

Hank Perlman: "Well, we've been having all kinds of computer problems in Accounting and everything's been backing up."

A/R Agent: "Yes, I recall. You told me you were having similar problems when we talked last time. You said you would write a check manually and mail it right away."

Hank Perlman: "Oh yeah, I remember. I think that must've gone out late last week. If you haven't gotten it by Friday, send me a copy of the invoice and I'll do some checking."

A/R Agent: "Okay, then I'll look for it sometime next week."

What are the chances that Mr. Perlman will ever pay his bill? How many more calls and letters will it take before this account is written off? Are the people who owe you money outwitting your Accounts Receivable clerks, or is the staff simply not very effective on the phone?

It's hard to believe that these people are all making use of the world's most powerful communications tool, the telephone.

Miscommunication, wasted time, emotional stress, and poor manners characterize most phone communications in business today. We've come to expect inefficiency and frustration. When calling other businesspeople, we just go through the motions. Perhaps we'll "get lucky," but more likely, we're merely making our next move in another round of "phone tag." When you call the shipping department and a clerk says, "I'll try to have him call you back after lunch," do you believe it?

The world's most enormous communications network seems poorly connected. The wires and satellites and PBXs are all in place. But *we* all seem to be on different channels. And yet, *some* people consistently get powerful, profitable results with their phones. *You* can be one of them.

Turn *your* telephone into a profit-producing power tool. Saving phone time, and increasing effectiveness, are simply matters of training and technique. We all use the telephone and we can all learn telephone skills that help us get more done.

Whether you are the receptionist or the president of a company, a busy consumer, or an anxious job seeker, your telephone is probably so taken for granted that you hardly pause to question whether there's a way you could use it more effectively. In fact, you *could* accomplish twice as much in half the time with the right telephone techniques.

How much training in phone communications has your organization offered its employees? Few of us know how to exploit the special features of our phone hardware, let alone master the human factors necessary to truly get them working for us.

There is no single activity American businesspeople spend more time doing (and less time improving) than using the telephone. Upper-level managers spend twice as much time phoning as they spend doing paperwork or reading. Even though it seems we're always in those dreaded "scheduled meetings," they actually account for 31 percent *less* time than phone calls. Executives frequently complain about mail deluges, but the truth is that they spend two and a half times as many hours handling phone calls as handling mail.

The only business tools used more intensively than the phone are pen or pencil and paper. As a business ally, a tool that should help us get much more accomplished, the telephone is sorely undervalued. It suffers the Rodney Dangerfield affliction: "No respect!"

We assume that we're using the phone effectively. Yet, the average business executive wastes five to seven hours each week playing phone tag, talking with callers who should have been screened, and wishing muddled, long-winded talkers would "get to the point." You may attempt thirty calls each day, but according to AT&T, fewer than eight are successful connections on the first try. The time we're all wasting translates into big money. There *is* a better way! You *can* use your telephone more profitably. This book will help you turn that undervalued desktop appliance into your most powerful business ally.

1

PHONE TAG: AVOID BEING "IT"

John Naisbitt introduced the notion of "information float" in his blockbuster, *Megatrends*. "Float" refers to the lag time between sending a message and receiving it. The most "mega" trend affecting our society today, Naisbitt contends, is the shift from an industrial-based society to one based on the exchange of information. Communications technologies have rapidly evolved in the last few decades, and particularly the last few years, so that the float period is collapsing. Information exchange today can be virtually instantaneous—unless we get trapped playing "phone tag."

Phone tag is a game known to—and despised by—all in business. But you don't have to play if you apply some basic disciplines:

SCHEDULING CALLS

Just as you schedule other key tasks through the day, allocate time for your phone calls. Get in the habit of reserving specific hours each day for the outbound calls you initiate, and for the callback responses you expect from others.

One of the most effective methods for short-circuiting phone tag is to make appointments to call. I suggest a preliminary call from your secretary to your contact's secretary. Schedule a specific time just as if it were an in-person appointment. Then, when you reach the part of your day blocked for phoning, you will have appointments prescheduled. Packets of background information, as detailed in Chapter 3, will be in order, and you will simply tick off the calls as you achieve your objectives. You (and your secretary) can both get out of the habit of scheduling vague callbacks. Go beyond "Have him call me when he gets back." Indefinite requests merely support the frustrating game.

> "I'll call Jesse again this afternoon. Two-thirty is a convenient time for me, or we can make it at four. Which better fits Jesse's schedule?"

You can do the same thing when scheduling the other person's callback. You're better off making calls in the active mode, but sometimes you must take the reactive position and handle a call on the other guy's turf. Rather than saying, "Have him call me," be more specific:

> "I've reserved from three to four o'clock this afternoon for callbacks. What time in that hour is most convenient for Jesse? I'll be expecting his call and we won't get caught playing phone tag."

My secretary helps me maximize my phone time and avoid phone tag by keeping an appointment sheet for callbacks. If you call my office from the Eastern U.S., she'll automatically set an appointment for the next morning between 10:00 and 11:00, your time. At the end of my day in California, she gives me this schedule of the next morning's call I'm to make from 7:00 to 8:00, my time. You're expecting my call, we don't get worn down playing phone tag, and I benefit from very low long distance charges during early morning hours. She schedules my local callbacks from 1:00 to 2:00 in the afternoon.

I always prefer to be the caller instead of the callee. We accomplish more, faster, when I have my agenda and notes in front of me and am mentally prepared to pursue an objective.

Sometimes I *have* to be the callee in order to end phone tag. But I'll only address a serious call when it has been scheduled in advance. That way, my secretary is alerted to expect the call and we're able to dive right into the business at hand.

Coca-Cola's manager of industry and consumer affairs, Roger Nunley, terminates games of phone tag by his sheer determination. When there's someone he's expecting to hear from, he alerts his secretary to watch for the call and track him down—even if he's in the men's room!

Another method, the "time-bomb" technique, can terminate phone tag altogether. The message you leave may say,

> "Please tell John that we will file the plan in its present form on Friday unless he calls by noon Thursday. Please be sure he understands that we will proceed as agreed unless he calls to make a change."

SECRETARIES AND MESSAGES

We all unconsciously perpetuate phone tag by giving and leaving messages like: "Just tell him I called," and "Have her call me back later." Secretaries can effectively short-circuit endless phone-tag loops by consistently asking for and giving specific messages. The rule of thumb is simple: Never use vague terms like "Call again later." Always cite a specific time and day when you'll be available to receive a call, or when you'll call back.

STEP AHEAD

Whether it's leaving better messages or making sure that you arrange a specific callback time, the name of the game in ending phone tag is to achieve the objective of getting a step closer with each call. Very often, it will be necessary to make several calls before completing a connection. Rather than simply crossing your fingers and hoping, make sure that every call consciously takes you one step closer to the desired conversation.

Take steps to end phone tag yourself:

Ask the secretary to have your party paged. Very often, he's right there in the same building. Simply taking this extra step will produce the conversation immediately.

Ask if there is another number where he can be reached. Your aim is to end phone tag, not cut back on phone bills. Remember, your time, the opportunity cost of "information float," and the mental muddling of delayed conversations all cost you much more than another phone call. Find out if your contact is merely in another building or office. Perhaps you can complete the contact right now.

Ask who handles the area of responsibility you are concerned with. It may be that the person you are calling would have referred you on anyway. The conversation you've been having trouble arranging may be completely unnecessary. Go directly to the right person.

TECHNOLOGICAL TAG STOPPERS

The key to ending phone tag is personal action. It's your persistent dedication to stepping-ahead strategies that's most important in solving this time- and energy-draining problem. But help is available. A trio of technological tools offers tremendous power in stopping the game. Although costly voice mail systems are getting the most attention, personal computers and even answering machines can help.

VOICE MAIL

Next to the introduction of personal computers throughout American business, no office technology has a more promising growth outlook than voice mail. The techno-hoopla is surprising, since voice mail, in its most primitive form, has been available for decades. Anybody with an answering machine has a "voice mailbox." These recorders have been viewed with scorn by most, and their application has been largely limited to residential use.

Most businesspeople are skeptical about voice mail because they personally hate leaving messages on other people's answering machines. Several years ago these same feelings applied to using automated tellers instead of banking with real live human tellers. But we've not only accepted automated tellers, we often prefer their efficiency to standing in line and hoping we end up with a well-trained employee. Companies using voice mail systems often find that their employees prefer leaving succinct messages to conversing with talkative peers.

Today voice mail is sweeping the American office scene. Modern systems use an array of "mailboxes" available to hundreds or thousands of users throughout the world. Conceptually, voice mail systems are like large closets filled with very smart answering machines, each bearing the "address" of a specific user.

There's no tape involved. The caller's voice is electronically broken down into millions of binary information bits. The "digitized" voice is then stored on a computer's hard-disk system. When you or a caller retrieve messages, the computer's sophisticated program decodes this digital information and translates it back into an exact duplicate of the original spoken message. It doesn't sound "synthesized"; it's indistinguishable from the original voice. (In fact, people using my system tell me that it sounds better than the "real me"!)

The biggest advantage of voice-mail systems is that they slash the "information float."

Small systems now add just a few hundred dollars to the cost of a PC. Although the large, sophisticated voice mail systems cost hundreds of thousands of dollars to install initially, the relevant cost is the per-user/per-day figure, and that's often less than a dollar. For a dollar per-person, per-day, here's what you get:

Twenty-four-hour accessibility. Although you may be out of town or in a meeting (or asleep), your mailbox is ready and waiting. Callers in other time zones can always get word through to you and it's available immediately when they are. This feature alone can dramatically reduce telecommunications costs. Business can be handled during off-peak hours when phone rates plummet by two-thirds or more. Randy Fields, president of the holding company that oversees more than 180 Mrs. Fields Cookies stores, estimates that his Rolm PhoneMail system has cut the corporate phone bill by 25 to 30 percent. The company policy is that every single store calls the system every night (even weekends) between 6 P.M. and 8 A.M., when rates are low.

The death of phone tag. Rather than endlessly swapping messages because you want to get a question answered and the person with the answer is unavailable, you call the voice-mail system and leave your question in the other person's mailbox. The person who has or can get the answers works at his convenience and—when available—leaves the answer in your voice mailbox. At Mrs. Fields, ". . . we at corporate now follow the dictum, 'Thou shalt not interrupt the stores . . . and vice versa!' All of our conversations with the field go over PhoneMail. No more phone tag."

Personal message dissemination. Want to get a message to someone who has no voice-mail system? You've got a couple of options:

- Leave the message in your own mail system with a personal identification code for the intended recipient. When he or she calls, the computer plays your message only to the person entering the special, personal code.
- Or, put your computer to the task. It will doggedly dial the other guy day and night (or only during the hours you mercifully designate) and won't give up until the other party answers. Then, it'll play your message (decoding it from the digital form in which it was stored), wait for a response, and record it for your retrieval later.

Mass message dissemination. A sales manager can record the Monday morning pep talk and market update for all sales reps around the country. Reps can call the central mailbox and hear the identical message whenever they're ready (and have finished their golf games), or the system can relentlessly call them each individually and deliver the message. Or better yet, the manager can simply record the message once, and then direct the system to place a copy in each salesman's box.

Dictation pools. "Marsha, please bring in your steno pad" is something we won't be hearing much longer. Now, we can call the word-processing pool's mailbox, dictate, playback, insert additional thoughts, selectively erase, change words, and so on, all without touching a piece of paper or tape recorder. And of course, we can do it from a pay phone at O'Hare Airport as easily as from the den at home, or from the office.

Technologically speaking, no tool is nearly as effective as voice mail when it comes to ending phone tag.

Implementation of sophisticated technologies isn't always smooth. Top management people must be the bellwether users. At Lotus, it took a "Save a Tree" memo from the president to get the ball rolling. (Some organizations report a 90 percent drop in intraoffice memos. That'll save a forest when we all use voice mail.) The folks at Lotus still talk about the first month when they were on the system. A top executive was recording his standard telephone greeting when someone walked into his office with a shocking item. He put his handset down in mid-sentence and thought no more about it. But he wondered why people leaving him messages always began with a chuckle. It was two weeks before he discovered that all who called him heard the greeting, "Hello, this is . . . Oh, shi—."

When Manhattan Life Insurance started using voice mail, a clerk accidentally discovered the "Distribute to Top Management" feature. He'd intended to leave a personal message for a friend, but accidentally hit a combination of buttons that dispatched his intimate message to all VPs and higher. Since every user has password protection on his own box, the unfortunate clerk could not retrieve or erase the accident.

PERSONAL COMPUTERS AND YOUR PHONE

A microcomputer, or PC, will revolutionize just about everything else in your office, why not your phone? As a telephone
time saver, nothing can beat the specialized phone management software and hardware available today.

The system I use is a commercially available product named
Watson. What it does to help me save time on the phone is
amazing. My typical phoning session goes like this:

When I come into the office, my PC screen displays a stack
of Rolodex-like cards that constitute my personal phone directory. Each shows the name and phone number of a colleague,
and they're automatically organized in alphabetical order. I
can always add information to each card by typing it in; for
example, a secretary's name, notes from a past conversation, a
change of address.

Let's say I want to call my editor this morning. I simply type
in her name, and the computer sorts through the hundreds of
cards to find her. Then I see a display of her card on top of the
stack. I hit a single key on the computer's keyboard and it dials
the call automatically.

This system is so smart that I may list several numbers for
each person, along with the hours when each is applicable. The
work number may be valid only from nine to five. The record
may also show a home number that's in effect from six to
midnight. There could even be a third number for her weekend
cottage that's in effect from Friday night to Monday morning.
Whatever the time, the computer automatically selects the applicable phone number and dials it. I never look up phone
numbers or figure out where someone is likely to be. I never
reach for the phone and punch in numbers. And I never misdial, thanks to Watson and my PC.

Likely as not, Adrienne's line is busy. So, of course, the
computer will continually redial until it gets through. Meanwhile, I'm idly sifting through junk mail or skimming through a
magazine. I might even head off to the coffee machine.

Wouldn't you know it? Just as I'm pouring the brew, the call
goes through. My computer notices that I haven't picked up

the phone to talk, so it announces to my editor (in my digitized voice) that "I'll be right there, just hold on for a moment, please." Cup in hand, I pick up the handset. The screen is signaling me that the call has been answered, and it even reminds me of who I called.

Nope, it's not Adrienne. Joe, her assistant, tells me that she's in an editorial review board meeting until noon. I ask Joe to have her call me. As we talk, the computer's timer shows me how many seconds I've been connected. If Joe were long-winded (which he definitely is not), I would be constantly aware of exactly how much valuable time he was gobbling.

Naturally, I plan to be out of the office at noon, so I know that we won't be able to talk when her meeting ends.

After Joe hangs up, I go ahead and talk to Adrienne, even though she's not on the line. The computer digitizes my voice, breaking it into millions of "bits," binary information that is stored on its disk. I tell her all that's on my mind, ask a few questions, and remind her to have a great weekend. And I leave the office.

Her meeting breaks up and Joe gives her the message to call me. When she does, my computer answers with a recorded message (in my voice) and asks her to punch in her prearranged ID code from her phone's Touch-Tone keypad. Doing so sends my computer on a split-second search of its disk looking for the message I recorded for her earlier. She hears my questions and answers them. Her voice is also broken down into digital form and stored on the disk. There's one point Adrienne wants to explore further, so she asks me to call her Sunday afternoon at her cottage.

When I return to the office, there's Adrienne's card on top of the stack displayed on my monitor screen. It tells me exactly when she called, how long she talked, and it can even display information she "typed" into her phone while leaving the message. The numbers that she pushes on her Touch-Tone keypad will appear as printed information in the visual record on my screen. My message could, for example, ask for her grandmother's telephone number and ask her to punch it in so it appears on my screen. If I were to call her there during

Grandma's dinner, I could do so automatically from the number she "keyed in."

I touch one button on my machine and I hear Adrienne's voice answering each question. And I also hear her ask me to call her on Sunday.

Now, I've got a weakness for champagne brunches on Sundays. I don't always remember every little thing on Sunday afternoons. So right now, on my office PC, I set a reminder appointment for 2 P.M. Sunday. I record myself a message in my own voice. "Have a cup of coffee and remember to call Adrienne." But this Sunday, I'm not going into the office. So I simply instruct Watson to call me at home, repeatedly at five-minute intervals, starting at 2 P.M. And when I answer, I will hear my own voice reminding me of the appointment. (While I'm at it, I record an anniversary message for my wife. Watson will call her at home with my singing greeting each April 6 from now till the end of the century.)

PC-based phone management systems save phone time by:

- keeping track of your entire telephone directory.
- dialing phone numbers automatically.
- selecting the number where your contact is most likely to be reached.
- eliminating the possibility of a misdial.
- automatically and persistently redialing if a number is busy.
- allowing you to proceed with other tasks while it's busy dialing for you.
- acting as a supersophisticated answering machine that leaves personal messages available only to the individuals you designate.
- allowing you to accomplish your business and get answers to your questions without coordinating your schedule with the other person's.
- speeding up the callback process so that you can instantly dial any individual who has left you a message.
- scheduling reminders for future tasks.

The ability to add this level of sophistication to your telephone management alone justifies buying and using a PC.

Undeniably, the most effective business calls are personal. But when time is at stake, a comprehensive recorded message delivered by a system like Watson is far preferable to a stack of pink "While You Were Out" message forms indicating more endless games of telephone tag are about to begin.

ANSWERING MACHINES

Even a $50.00 answering machine will offer a significant advantage when you're out to end the phone tag game. Yes, many of your calls require conversation and give-and-take, but many are questions or quick answers. These can be efficiently handled once with a taped message rather than a series of failed callbacks.

The pervasive use of these inexpensive devices for residential applications has paved the way for business uses. We've all become accustomed to using the machines and most of us have overcome stage fright. Some of us actually prefer a quick exchange with a machine to a more personal but time-consuming conversation.

When selecting a machine, look for these valuable features:

- Variable message length so that you aren't locked into a 30 or 60 second tape. The beep will sound when you want it to.
- Voice activated recording so you'll record your caller as long as he speaks, but won't record dial tones when callers hang up.
- Beeperless remote retrieval so you can pick up your messages without returning to your office. It's best to get a machine that allows you to change your announcement message remotely, too. The beeperless models eliminate the need to carry a small, battery-powered device. You can command the answering machine with the buttons on any Touch-Tone phone.

Not many people have taken the simple, inexpensive step of putting an answering machine to work in their offices. But it's not surprising. Not many people have taken *any* steps to short-circuit their games of phone tag.

The death of phone tag results only from conscious effort. All the high-tech toys in the world aren't going to eliminate the problem unless you determine to change it on both ends—yours and everyone else's.

When you place five calls to your banker and at the end of the week still haven't been able to reach him *or* gotten a return call, what's your reaction? Either the bank is completely disorganized and your banker hasn't even gotten the message to call you, or he doesn't consider you important enough to phone back. Maybe after three days, he's so embarrassed by all the late, later, latest callbacks he owes that he procrastinates further. At any rate, he's making himself look—and feel—worse all the time.

Don't do it to yourself. End phone tag by following the Golden Rule. Return your calls as you'd like calls returned to you. The impression conveyed when you pay prompt attention to your callbacks is that you are conscientious, professional, and reliable.

2
OPENING DOORS: EASE THROUGH ANY LABYRINTH

The most frustrating and most time-wasting phone situation is confronting a confusing, disorganized, perhaps hostile bureaucracy. Intentionally or not, the whole organization may seem bent on blocking your contact. It's not always the result of indifference, as with the monopolistic utility companies or government agencies. Sometimes, even people who want to talk to us have built-in "blocks" that make contact nearly impossible.

I recently got a call from a major forklift company in Southern California. The name rhymes with "Scheister." They called because they were seeking information about telemarketing training opportunities. I wasn't available when the call came in, but I did return it the next morning.

The main number rang twenty times (I counted) before anyone answered. A receptionist hurriedly blurted something I couldn't decipher. It sounded like "High Sill Company," and that didn't match the name on my message slip. I asked for Jeff Oscar by name. Without a word, I was transferred to an unidentified extension. It rang eight times before the operator returned with a hurried "One moment" and then more ringing. Again, eight rings.

Again, the operator returned with a quick "One moment" before switching me to a recording. A radio announcer voice came on the line and began telling me how convenient the company's one-stop "Unisource" parts program was. I couldn't believe it. Here I was, being anonymously bounced from extension to extension, and this taped message had the gall to boast about how convenient it was to do business with the company.

Eventually, the operator returned and informed me that she wasn't getting an answer on Jeff's line. No kidding! I left a message for him to call me.

Next morning, my curiosity was piqued. Jeff hadn't called. I wondered if I had just experienced a particularly bad day. So I called again.

Again, the indistinguishable answer. Then the perfunctory transfer to Jeff's extension. (Remember, this is the convenient, one-stop company.) It rang, and rang, and I counted again just to appease my curiosity. *Thirty-four rings!* Had someone laced the office coffeepot with cyanide? Wouldn't any living person walk over and answer Jeff's phone after twenty or thirty jangling, distracting rings? Finally the operator returned to the line and very quickly with a "One moment please" put me through to the boasting tape again.

Believe it or not, after several minutes of golden-voiced announcements ("Good news! We're happy to announce a special sale on reconditioned fleet forklifts"), who should answer but Jeff Oscar himself!

I answered Jeff's telemarketing question and then gave him some feedback about my difficulties in reaching him. He said he was glad that I'd brought it to his attention. Although his company was the worst I've encountered, lots of organizations are almost as bad.

PENETRATING SCREENS

Getting through a tangled bureaucracy or disorganized company, or stalking an elusive individual who assumes that your conversation won't be worthwhile, involves using strategy. Success awaits those who play the strategy game rather than simply flinging themselves repeatedly against closed doors until they either collapse from frustration and exhaustion or break through.

YOUR INFORMATION RESOURCE

The starting point in any penetration strategy is the switchboard. In most organizations, unsolicited calls reach a central operator or switchboard who normally acts as a simple switch. He does little more than connect you with the requested extension. Ask your receptionist how many people he talks with each day. The answer may be 250 or more. But how many people does he *really* talk with each day—converse beyond a quick "Extension 322, please"—and the number plummets. Maybe two or three people actually regard this voice as a person rather than a human switching device. Therein lies the opportunity.

Busy as they are, switchboard people get little real human interaction on the phone. Many are actually lonely. And they can also be a fount of valuable information—if you tap them. You may think that these front-liners are too busy to chat. I know that's not true because of Beverly. Dear Beverly was a child star in the 1950s movie *Old Yeller* and years later handled the switchboard of the large ad agency where I worked for five years. Beverly is the kind of person who doesn't just sit back and feel lonely. She actively makes friends on the phone and actually carried on many extended conversations while competently covering a very busy switchboard.

Bev was always available for a long, gossipy chat. And as long as incoming business calls got prompt, professional attention, she had the implicit blessing of the office manager to talk with whomever she wished. Her friends became completely accustomed to conversations that went like this: ". . . and then he brought out this small dog, it was one of those—I've got a call . . . one of those little yipping ones with—just a sec . . . with pink bows and teeth that jutted out too far—got another call . . . and he actually threw it in—hang on . . . he threw it in the—hold on . . . right in the pool! And he said to me—just a sec . . ."

With the right approach, a well-phrased question, and some patience, you can converse with a switchboard operator. Regard her or him as an information resource and approach this knowledgeable person in a friendly, human way.

And here's what you want to find out: *"I know you're very busy, so put me on hold whenever you need to. Please tell me . . .*

. . . who's the person responsible for purchasing supplies?" You don't care about organization charts. You want the practical, day-to-day reality. And the switchboard operator is ideally situated to know who's really doing what. If you don't even know with whom you should speak, the operator can help.

. . . who does she report to?" And if you really want to heighten your chance of reaching the intended party, call that person's boss first. Suppose you sell cleaning supplies and the person who can specify your product is Earl Lerner, the cleaning supervisor. If Earl reports to Hank Wynn, the facilities manager, call Hank first. Undoubtedly, you'll be referred back to the cleaning supervisor. But now, you may call and say, "I've been referred by Hank Wynn. Is Earl available, please?" You're in a much stronger position and far more likely to gain immediate attention. It's the old "top down" approach salespeople have always used effectively.

Don Thompson, a VP at Avery International, was having a hard time garnering research from the glassware industry when Avery decided to produce special labels for pharmaceutical jars. His troubles ended when he began calling the presidents of the glass companies. They didn't know the answers, but when Don was transferred from the president to the clerks who had the figures, the floodgates opened; no more tooth-pulling!

. . . how is his name pronounced?" You should try to avoid any gaffe that you can. And what worse way to begin a conversation than by mangling someone's name? Get pronunciation cleared up with the operator, before you reach your target's secretary.

. . . what is his secretary's name?" Everybody loves to hear her own name, secretaries included. And it's also helpful to create the impression that you are already acquainted. "Hello, Janet? Janet, this is George Walther. Will you put Mort on please?"

. . . does she usually come in early or stay late?" If you're attempting to connect with an elusive but influential busi-

nessperson, you can be pretty sure that she doesn't work nine-to-five hours. The operator may say, "Early or late? Why, Joanne must get here at sunrise." Now you know when to call. Whenever possible, call at a time when your call won't be competing with dozens of other intrusions. And you're also best off calling when the individual's secretary isn't guarding the gates. Calling before or after regular working hours will often get you right through to your intended contact.

. . . *what's usually the best time to call that department?"* Simple question, valuable answer. Often, you'll get a response that not only helps you get through, but also helps your intended contact get through the day. "Accounting? They're insane all day on Fridays and mornings are pretty hectic, too. You're best off calling early in the week just after lunch."

Obviously, you won't *always* find a helpful switchboard operator. But even if you do only half the time, you're way ahead of the game. And most organizations have more than one operator. If there's only one operator, there's always a relief person working during lunch. Call again then.

END-RUNNING

You'd always prefer to get straight through to the boss, so first take that approach. Your best shot is to call when the "screen" isn't in place. Secretaries rarely work the same hours as their bosses, so try early in the morning, or after most office workers have left but the execs are still plugging along. If you're lucky, the person you're after will answer her own phone.

The Los Angeles Times calls Jerry Asher the "Maestro of Real Estate." He's the senior vice president of Coldwell Banker, the biggest real estate brokerage in America. He recently put together $441 million dollars in sales of the principal buildings of the Century City development in Los Angeles. Fresh out of the Army, Jerry heard about real estate magnate Bill Zeckendorf and decided he wanted to work for and learn from this big player. He read several articles about Zeckendorf and discovered that he liked getting to work very early. Asher was in Los Angeles, Zeckendorf in New York. Every day for a week, Asher set his alarm for three thirty in the morning so he could call Zeckendorf as he walked into the office at six thirty, New York time.

"For five solid days, I let the phone ring and ring. Finally, somebody answered; it was Zeckendorf."

The result? In short order, Asher became part of Zeckendorf's team. The rest is real estate history.

You may also use the presumptive approach when the secretary does intercept. Adopt the attitude that you have valuable information and that the target will want to talk with you. Presume that you'll get through. And let that presumptive attitude carry through with your voice and word choice.

What won't work:

"Hello. I'm a salesman for Exmet Chemicals and we have a complete line of cleaning chemicals. I wonder if I could possibly take a few minutes of Mr. Chordman's time. Is he busy right now?"

What may work:

"Hi, Susan? This is John Welsh. Is Harold there, please?"

Understand that John Welsh may be a perfect stranger and still use this approach quite effectively. First, he asks the switchboard operator for the proper pronunciation of Harold Chordman's name. He also asks who Harold's secretary is. Then he calls at an off-prime hour. If he doesn't get directly through to Harold, there's still a good chance that the person who answers won't be Mr. Chordman's regular secretary. She may be at lunch, or otherwise away from her desk. If someone else does intercept the call, this presumptive approach is likely to succeed. She doesn't know who you are, but you sound like you should be put through.

OPPONENT OR ALLY?

Some heavy phoners, unscrupulous salespeople in particular, will do anything to barge past the secretary. I find it much more effective to use her as an ally. Start with the assumption that your reason for calling is to find an opportunity for both you and the person you're calling to come out ahead. (If that's not truly the case, you probably shouldn't be calling anyway.) And then realize that the secretary's function is to help the boss sort out which calls offer genuine opportunities. She's to screen out all the others. With this approach, the secretary really is your ally. You and she both want to find opportunities for the boss. The problem lies in communicating the nature of the call in such a way that you do get through. As with all other phone encounters, there are two primary matters on the agenda: personal, emotional feelings (this time involving the secretary) and the objective facts about the call.

THE PERSON COMES FIRST

Begin with the person. Secretaries deserve tons of respect. Not just because they're usually deeply involved in turning the wheels of business, but also because they can get you through or blackball you.

Do everything possible to create rapport. Like the boss, the secretary also likes hearing her own name. Use her name. And, of course, note it for your records. I always add a comment to help me recognize the voice on future calls. "Husky sounding, slight New England accent," "very quiet, sounds young," and so forth.

I recently called a Washington, D.C., consultant and asked his secretary's name. Marlene. Bingo! That's my sister's name. Each time I call, there's room for a little comment.

My accountant, Dale Rozzen, has to deal with the most frustrating of bureaucracies, the IRS. I recall sitting in his office while he called to resolve a long-standing dispute about a corporate tax discrepancy. The problem resolution officer who answered was Ms. Routz. Dale immediately started in with,

"Boy, am I glad I got *you*. My name's Dale Rozzen and I've always found that people with z's in their names are the smartest." It broke the ice and Dale established a contact. The problem bounced around for months, and each time Dale called, he quickly got on a friendly footing with a quick, "Remember me? I'm the guy who also has a 'z' name."

During one extended negotiation, I encountered a particularly helpful secretary. We spoke fourteen times before I connected with the publishing executive I wanted to talk with at CBS/Fox Video. It would have been easy for Jane to get fed up with my persistent calls. She was genuinely doing her best to get two very busy people connected. So I jotted out a quick handwritten note thanking her for being patient. She deserved the recognition. I felt good about acknowledging her help. And I did ultimately get through.

Speaking of appreciation, praise and thanks are the two most underutilized emotional tools in the world. Everybody loves to hear something nice. We all nod and say, "Yeah, Ken Blanchard was right in *One-Minute Manager,* it really pays to 'catch someone doing something right.'" But who does it?

Secretaries, switchboard operators, and other phone pros get lots of heat and not much appreciation. I make it a point, every day, to notice and reward at least one telephone professional who handles my call well. Sometimes it's a Federal Express dispatcher, sometimes it's a Marriott Hotels reservations agent, sometimes a client's secretary. I tell the person specifically what I appreciated about the way my call was handled. And then I ask if I may let the supervisor know how I feel. I haven't been turned down yet.

You may dismiss this as do-good fluff. "Is he serious? I'm supposed to tell the United Airlines agent that he did a nice job of searching out a discounted fare for me? And then I'm supposed to talk to the supervisor? Come on . . ." That's exactly what I'm saying. Every time I comment positively on someone's telephone technique, four things happen. Sometimes five.

1. *I feel good.* Simple and true. I get a great rush from telling somebody that his techniques are noticed and appreciated.
2. *He feels good.* Maybe this is a little on the altruistic side, but doesn't excellence deserve a reward?
3. *I help the supervisor.* As a manager, I'm always grateful for feedback about my employees. I'm sure she will be, too.
4. *I stay focused on what I like.* Also, the techniques I like in others, others like in me. When I keep my finger on my own pulse, I learn what turns me on. I can then do the same things to be more effective when I talk with others.
5. *And sometimes, something neat and unexpected happens.* I get handled better on the next call. Once I reported a United Airlines Mileage Plus agent for doing a great job. Somehow, 5,000 bonus miles showed up in my account. I once expressed appreciation to a Kodak customer service rep and found free film in my mailbox the following week. When I complimented the folks at Long Distance Roses, I ended up with a dozen.

AND NOW THE FACTS

Brief, brief, brief. Give the secretary only enough information to whet her and her boss's appetite. The key word is "benefits." Specific benefits. Tell her how the boss will come out ahead, or why it is to her advantage to talk with you. Don't call and say, "I'm calling because I'd like to tell you about our maintenance agreements on office copiers." The stronger approach is, "I'm calling because I may be able to save you fifteen to thirty-five percent on the maintenance costs for your office copiers. I'll be able to give Mr. Johnson a good idea of just how much he can save by asking him four questions. For your machines, that means annual savings somewhere between $1200 and $2800. Can we schedule a ten-minute call this afternoon, or is tomorrow morning better?"

Show the secretary that your call presents an opportunity for the boss to come out ahead. And then keep focused on a specific objective: get through now, or set a specific, confirmed appointment when you'll both be geared up for the call.

SETTING ASSUMPTIVE APPOINTMENTS

There's no way around it: first calls frequently will not get through. The enervating part of penetrating is the ongoing repeat attempts. The only two ways to get through the impenetrable front lines of agencies and corporations are to:

- increase the odds of getting through the first time, and
- reduce the number of repeat attempts by making them more effective.

To cut the number of repeat attempts, be sure that you always make an appointment to call, rather than just trying again later. Suppose a secretary takes your call and tells you that the executive you want to reach is out of town all week.

"John, will Elaine be in on Monday? She'll probably want a day to get caught up, so I'll be glad to call on Tuesday. Are mornings generally better, or is she less tied up in the afternoon? Fine, I'll call at two-thirty, if that looks clear. John, will you please note on your calendar that I'll be calling? I'll ask the switchboard to put me right through on Elaine's line at two-thirty next Tuesday."

I'm not suggesting that Elaine will be hovering over the phone at 2:29 waiting for your call. But you do stand a better chance of reaching her by setting the appointment. And even if you don't reach her then, you do create a determined, professional image by following through as scheduled.

MAILING SYNERGY

When two actions work together to produce a result more powerful than the sum of its parts, the effect is called synergy. Mail and phone calls, working together to reinforce each other, present a great opportunity for synergy. When scheduling an appointment for a future callback, put synergy to work by sending a written confirmation of the appointment. This helps to avoid possible conflicts by reminding the secretary to check his calendar, and it also elevates the seriousness of your commitment.

You could simply print up some postcards that read:

I look forward to talking with you, as scheduled, on _____ at _____. If anything comes up and you want to schedule for a more convenient time, please give me a call. Until then,

Or, if you are using a PC at your desk, be sure to take advantage of the Rolodex-style programs that keep track of names, phone numbers, and addresses. After completing your scheduling, it takes just a few seconds to generate a professional confirmation letter. The program will retrieve the name and address from its file and merge them with your standard letter, inserting the appropriate scheduled time and date.

Sometimes you have to get more creative when using the mail to reinforce an oral agreement. I recall my early contacts with Nightingale-Conant Corporation, the world's largest publisher of nonmusic audiocassettes. I wanted to author a program for them and was eager to move ahead. I'd made my proposal and could see no reason to delay. I was a bit overzealous and applied too much pressure in suggesting an immediate visit to Chicago.

My contact, Nick Carter, said, "Slow down, now. Let me tell you how things work around here. We've got a big ol' stove down the hall with several kettles simmering on it. When we start considering a new program, we put it in a kettle and let it kind of boil for a while. Each time we pass the stove, we give the kettles a sniff. If they start to smell like money, we move ahead. But it's a slow process and you really can't rush us. If you want to call in a couple of weeks, I'll let you know if anything has changed."

I felt pretty sure that this was a brush-off, but jotted the date in my calendar anyway. Producing the program meant a lot to me, and I knew I could do a great job for this publisher. I was determined to make it happen. I headed off to one of those import stores that carries lots of candles and rattan furniture. Sure enough, they stocked some very large carved wooden spoons that Mexicans supposedly use to stir huge kettles of frijoles.

Thirteen days later, Nick Carter received an oversized Federal Express pouch with a large spoon and a short note:

> Nick, tomorrow will be two weeks. Go down the hall and give the kettle a stir and a sniff. I will call at 10:00 A.M., your time. Let me know how it smells.

Nick took my call, said it smelled good, and that I should get a flight to Chicago. Just weeks later, they locked me in the studio and the cassette album became the fastest-selling training tapes in the telemarketing industry. I give much of the credit to the synergy created by that spoon and note.

PHONE TIME: ACCOMPLISH MORE IN LESS TIME

TIME IS AT THE TOP

When you hear mutterings about phone problems, they usually concern time. Everyone resents being robbed of this limited resource. We all want phone calls to be efficient but effective in building personal comfort, rapport, and respect. One of the surest ways to rub someone wrong is to take too long on the telephone.

Mark McCormack, author of *What They Don't Teach You at Harvard Business School,* puts it this way: "In business relationships, you have to be as conscious of other people's time as you would expect and hope they would be of yours." It's the old Golden Rule: Respect other people's time, and you will also be saving your own. And you'll eliminate the possibility of being judged an inconsiderate time thief.

I work with telephone professionals around the country in both public seminars and private consultations. They range from clerks at the U.S. Senate, to customer service representatives at used-car dealerships, to corporate executives at companies as large as Xerox to small-company presidents. Whether their jobs involve talking with venture capitalists or disgruntled citizens; whether their responsibilities are to handle complaints or to screen calls for senior executives, telephone professionals share exactly the same dominant concern: saving time.

I conduct an ongoing National Survey of Telephone Professionals who spend more than 50 percent of their workdays on the phone. The study reveals clear agreement on one point: *Time waste is the major problem.* When asked, "What one piece of advice would you give those people who call you at work? and at home?" these professionals respond as if in a chorus: "Get to the point! Clearly state your problem and your needs. Identify yourself and your company. Get on with it!"

TEAMING WITH TALENT

For a businessperson with a secretary, the biggest opportunity to save time comes from working more effectively together. Team up with your secretary and tap his or her phone talents. Your teammate's real function is to make it easy for you to accomplish more by eliminating interruptions and low-payoff work. Business executives underutilize their support resources. Your secretary should be your most powerful partner. And if you're not getting enough support now, take responsibility. Do something about it. Save time by reviewing the exact procedures you want your secretary to follow in handling your calls. And be sure that he or she offers ample input as you build a call-management system.

SCREENING YOUR CALLS

Many secretaries just don't screen calls. As a result, they merely impede communication and become a wrench in the works. Screening calls is a positive, double-win technique. An effective screening system will:

- help your callers get faster answers by directing them to the people best able to help them.
- save you hours of aggravation by eliminating the need to "brush off" people you really don't want to talk with.

- ensure that you are focused on the important calls, with background materials in hand, allowing you and the caller to get more accomplished, more quickly.
- give your secretary a more active, responsible role in communicating with callers.

There are three kinds of callers:

1. People you want to talk with. Of course, some are more important than others.
2. People you *don't* want to talk with, period. Get agreement with your secretary about which callers match your "pest" profile.
3. And people you're not sure about. If you had more information, you'd know.

BLESSED OR PEST?

Who are the few people so important that you want to be certain of connecting, regardless? Who should your secretary be extra courteous to, but never interrupt you for? Who should she turn away? Organizing callbacks is for your benefit, as well as the callers'. The other guy doesn't want to waste time playing phone tag any more than you do.

Your secretary's screening system should address all three situations:

"Hello, Mrs. Malcolm. I'm glad you called. Hank wants to talk with you and asked me to watch for your call. I'd like to schedule a callback so you can get connected. Is two-thirty this afternoon convenient, or is tomorrow morning better?"

"Mr. Roche, I can appreciate that you believe in your product and want to talk with Mr. Edwards, but we are completely happy with our present supplier and have no interest in changing. Mr. Edwards has specifically asked me not to interrupt him with sales calls."

"Mr. Cohen, Hank isn't available for phone calls right now, but I do work with him arranging callback schedules. Please tell me a little about your call and I'll do my best to help."

A great call screener blends investigative curiosity with complete courtesy. The objectives are to make certain that important callers do not get involved in games of phone tag with you and to ensure that your time isn't wasted on calls that you don't value.

MAKING MESSAGES MATTER

Dump those little pink "While You Were Out" pads. No secretary can effectively communicate all she's gleaned on three or four cramped lines. Custom design a message form that will meet your specific needs. These forms can give you an important "edge" in communicating with others.

Gathering Basic Facts   Of course, your message slip will include:

Name: But wouldn't it help to have a phonetic version right beside it so you don't start off on the wrong foot with Mieke Tsoucamangos?

Company/Organization: For companies you're not immediately familiar with, ask your secretary to jot a few words describing their business.

Phone Number: Do you recognize every area code? When the call is long-distance, ask for a time zone indication so you'll be able to schedule your call for the most likely connection.

When: Yes, it may be vital to know *exactly* when the call came in. Include time as well as the date.

Concerning: Nearly every message form has a space for describing the nature of the call, but we don't put it to work often enough. As a manager, you know that the behavior you reward gets repeated. Let your secretary know how much you value the "Concerning" comments. You'll notice a rapid increase in the number and quality of these helpful cues.

That's all the information the basic message form allows. But even these bare facts are rarely provided in any thorough fashion. "Concerning" is the first to go. Pretty soon, you face a stack of callback slips with little more than a scrawled name and phone number.

Getting an Edge   There are some extra elements of a message that, though rarely used, will definitely give you an "edge" when returning a call:

Emotions: Ask your secretary to use intuition. Your message is much more useful if you know whether the caller seemed agitated and irritated, or upbeat and friendly.

Promises: The surest way to diminish your esteem among others is to break promises. If your secretary said, "I'll be sure he reaches you before the end of the day," or "We'll get the replacement shipped today and call you with the airbill number this afternoon," you want a clear record to ensure follow-through.

Last Contact: Whenever possible, review copies of recent correspondence. If you and the caller have spoken before, when? About what? If you're anything like me, your secretary knows much more recent history than you do.

Impressions: I've been amazed at what my secretaries "pick up" in brief phone contacts. They get vital—and usually accurate—impressions that play a key role in shaping my approach on future calls. Your secretary is your partner and gains lots of information from "listening between the lines." All you have to do is ask for it.

You'll get helpful nuggets like:

"Didn't really sound terribly honest. Keep your guard up."

"Very friendly and nice. Gets right to the point without much B.S."

"Seems to want something from you. She's 'buttering me up' to pave the way."

"Sincere and professional. Listened carefully and communicated clearly. Probably worth talking with."

"When you call this customer back, ask him to give you a summary of main points. A real time thief!"

"Very warm person. Said nice things about you and remembered my name from last month's call."

WHAT'S IT WORTH?

The bedrock of effective time management is prioritizing tasks. Not all calls are of equal importance. Just as there are some jobs we'd rather do, there are some calls we'd rather make, even though they aren't the most important. The tendency to substitute preferences for priorities makes us accomplish less than we should.

Every message should bear a priority code. It may be very simple:

A: Act today. Important call.

B: Better today, but tomorrow morning is okay. Not an urgent call.

C: Cool; Return the call sometime when convenient.

D: Doesn't require action. Just letting you know about the call.

There's absolutely nothing tricky about setting up a priority system. The only hard part is habitually assigning a rank on every message and then handling callbacks accordingly and diligently.

Message Slip

Caller's Name: Priority: ☐
(Phonetic Spelling):
Company Name: City:
Type of Business:
Main Phone Number: (   )
Extension: Time Zone: AutoCode:
Alternate Number:

Most Recent Contact:
Main Purpose of This Call:

Evident Emotions/My Impressions:

To prepare for this callback, be sure to have:

Caller asked you to call back on _____ between _____ and _____.

Caller will call you again on _____ between _____ and _____.
I Promised:

		Date	Time
Attached:	Message Taken By: ____	____	____
☐ Recent Letters	Delivered To: ____	____	____
☐ Past Message Slips	Callback By: ____	____	____
☐ _____	File In: ____	____	____

PREPARING

Here's where you get the biggest payoff from teaming with your secretary. Most of the wasted time we rack up on the phone can be traced to inadequate preparation. Either we don't have materials at hand to record meaningful notes (and therefore must ask for the details when we call again), or we're rustling around in the files to get background information. Consult with your secretary and agree on a "preparation package" that will be attached to all important callback messages. Ask your secretary to:

Rank your callbacks. Literally, ask for them in the properly ordered sequence according to the agreed priorities. Don't even glance at the less important messages on the bottom until you've completed the priority calls. Get completely through the A's before touching the B's.

Attach past messages. A carefully designed message form incorporating the "edge" elements is an extremely powerful preparation tool. A quick scan of recent message forms will give you clues to emotional undercurrents and trigger your recall of vital details from past conversations. You're in a great position to offer comments—both personal and business—that reflect your recollections of earlier exchanges.

Retrieve recent correspondence. If copies of the last letter or two are attached, you're in an excellent position to prepare for the call by scanning them. Take a moment to refresh yourself about the details of recent contacts.

Clip a note-taking form on top of the package. This will encourage you to plan your objectives and strategies before speaking and to jot notes during the call.

Program your auto-dialer. If you use an auto-dialer for frequently called numbers, consider using its capabilities in another way. Your main objective is to off-load as much low-productivity work as possible. Have your secretary program unused positions in your auto-dialer so that, at callback time, punching a couple of buttons will immediately connect you. Your message/callback form may simply indicate the auto-dial code.

SECRETARIAL CHECKLIST

Secretaries, don't wait for your boss to do what's best for both of you. Most managers could do with a good bit of managing themselves. Take the reins. Inefficient phone procedures harm both you and your boss. Begin right now and list the major steps you can take toward cleaning up the ship.

Ask your boss for the "Blessed or Pest" list. This will take some coaxing. The list will grow and change with time, and you'll both be glad you started it.

Take the initiative in setting up a callback appointment schedule for your underorganized boss. You'll probably have to be assertive in order to pin him down each day. Again, you'll quickly find that the boss is grateful for your help and is very unlikely to say "Back off!" once he sees how much smoother things run with a callback schedule.

Redesign office message forms so that everyone gets complete information about their calls. Show your boss your prototype before putting it in final form. Working jointly, you'll come up with a very useful creation that will put the pink pads to shame. Don't print up a million; within a week you will each have several ideas to improve the forms. Make a quick trip to a local printer or your own reproduction department and have these glued together in pad form for convenience.

Gently encourage the boss to let you arrange an efficient "phone station." A very effective setup is described later in this chapter. It's only furniture and equipment and can always be returned to its original position. Forget your fears. What will really happen is that Big Boss will begin boasting to the others about how well you care for him.

Set up a message center for the office so that phones are always staffed and messages never slip through the cracks.

You know who butters your bread. If you want your career to advance, you've got to take things into your own hands. The surest way to get recognition and appreciation is to embark on a series of steps that will make your boss work more effectively.

INBOUND CALLS: THE HARDEST TO MANAGE

We don't just sit at our desks, hands poised over telephones, eagerly hoping someone will call. Inbound calls are almost always interruptions that distract us from other projects. Unfortunately, the inbound call forces you into a reactive mode. Your mind is on another project. You aren't tuned in. You don't have the proper preparation and materials to focus on the call.

Skilled negotiators and experienced telephone professionals always prefer to work on their own "turf." On the telephone, "turf" belongs to the person who dialed the phone. When you are the caller, you control the turf. By initiating the call, you've already determined *when* the conversation will take place. You have prepared and cleared your mind of distractions, so you have a natural advantage. Your attention is focused on achieving a primary written objective that's right in front of you.

The one who receives the call has a distinct disadvantage in managing the call. My recommendation? Take very few inbound calls. Your time will be best used if your secretary screens inbound calls, assembles preparation packets for you, and schedules the callbacks. You'll be able to accomplish much more, on your own terms, when you have all reference materials in hand and are calling on your own turf.

The toll charges you rack up by relying on outbound calls whenever possible are insignificant when compared with the bigger picture. Your more efficiently used time alone makes callbacks economically sensible. But the biggest advantage comes from your control of the turf. You are much more likely to achieve your objectives when you are in the active, outbound mode, focused on your objectives, and free from distractions.

HELPING THE CALLER USE YOUR TIME WELL

However bad you may be at managing your own phone time, the other guy is probably worse. Even when you must respond to an inbound call, you can still impose some waste-reducing tactics. If you were originating the call, you'd first outline the major subjects you wanted to cover. The person who has just called you is not likely to have done that. Do yourself and your caller a favor by outlining the call together. This saves time for you and the caller. You can say something like:

> "Hi, Don. I'm glad to hear from you. Will you give me a quick overview of the main points you want to cover today?"

Don't feel that just because the other guy called you you're prevented from imposing order where there may be none. And, certainly, use the outlining technique in the "Outbound Calls" section that follows.

One problem that afflicts both speakers and listeners is the failure to keep "on track" with one subject at a time. Frequently, the person who is calling you is wandering from point to point. You'll both benefit if you interrupt with:

> "Don, this sounds like another important point. Before we go on, I'd like to clarify a couple of details about the situation you were describing a minute ago . . ."

SETTING LIMITS

Assertiveness-training graduates often go limp on the phone. Stick up for your rights! It's amazing how often we respond untruthfully when the caller says, "Have you got a few minutes?" What he's actually asking is "Will you give me your full attention for a few minutes?" If the truth is no, say so! Tell the truth:

> "If it's something quick, Steve, let's cover it now. Otherwise, I'm focused on a writing project at the moment. I can give you my full attention for a few minutes later this afternoon."

If you've been asked for a "few minutes" and have consented, be ruthless about protecting your time:

> "Yes, I do have a *few* minutes, Bill, but I do have another commitment that starts at eleven-fifteen. What are the major points we need to cover?"

Ask your secretary to help protect the time you spend on incoming calls. The editor in chief of a large New York publishing house was responsible for the day-to-day operation of the firm and also personally edited several best-selling authors. Although his days were filled with meetings and managerial tasks, he gave his secretary a list of these important authors and their agents and instructed her to put their calls through even if it meant interrupting him.

When his authors called, the secretary would say, "Hello,

Nathan. Ted is in a meeting now, but I'm sure he'll take a few
minutes out now to speak with you. Please hold on while I get
him on the line."

His secretary had already established the limits for the call
and rarely did the callers take more than a few minutes.

OUTBOUND CALLS: LEVERAGING OPPORTUNITIES

We all want to spend a good part of our business day fostering
and nurturing relationships with colleagues, customers, clients,
and co-workers. But there's only so much time. The most efficient way to accomplish your objectives is to carefully organize
your outbound calls. This is the best way to squeeze maximum
results from every minute you invest using the phone.

BE PREPARED

Most wasted phone time occurs while you're off the phone!
The biggest time drain stems from incomplete or nonexistent
preparation. If you're not prepared to listen and record notes,
you'll most likely have to ask for a repeat later, when you are
prepared. If you need to put someone on hold while you fish
some recent letter out of a file, you're squandering your time
and the other guy's. If you're not assisted by a secretary, make
your own callback-preparation packet with recent phone messages, correspondence, and a note-taking form.

WRITTEN OBJECTIVES

Why do we prepare thoroughly for face-to-face meetings, but
expect to "wing it" on the phone? The fact that we spend lots
of time preparing for meetings and almost no time preparing
for phone calls is especially curious, since we do so much more
business on the phone than in meetings.

Your telephone can be your most profitable business tool,
but only if you use it effectively. You prepare for in-person

visits by planning your objectives and thinking about what you want to accomplish before the meeting gets underway. You should do the same thing with phone calls. Get your ducks in a row before placing any calls. You'll be far more likely to achieve your objectives.

One of the best time investments to hone your phone skills is to design a "Call Planning and Objectives Form." Very simply, this is an aid to organizing calls before placing them. It helps you to organize your thoughts, gives you a place to jot notes, and keeps you focused on the primary objective of your call. The key ingredient is the specific objective(s) you seek to achieve during a given call. This may be fairly loose, such as, "Let the customer know I am thinking of him, while piquing his interest about our new line coming in the fall." Or, you may set a more definite objective: "Schedule an appointment for

Call Planning and Objectives Form

Caller: Date   Time

Calling:

First Call   _____   _____

Scheduled 1st Callback   _____   _____

Company: Actual 1st Callback   _____   _____

Scheduled 2nd Callback   _____   _____

Call: (   ) _____-_____   Actual 2nd Callback   _____   _____

Scheduled 3rd Callback   _____   _____

Zone: _____   Actual 3rd Callback   _____   _____

Estimated Time Needed: _____ mins.

Primary Objective:

Secondary Objectives:

●

●

Bottom-Line Fallback:

Topics to Cover:

Key Questions to Raise:

our first in-person meeting during my Detroit trip next month."

Heighten the odds of achieving *some* level of success by listing secondary objectives, and even a "Bottom-Line Fall-back" objective. Resolve that, even if you aren't successful in achieving your first or second objectives, you *will* at least make some headway toward your long-range goal.

The "Call Planning and Objectives Form" is the place to record notes as you talk. Keep your focus on the objectives you're out to achieve and ensure that the call keeps moving in the right direction.

When you're effective on the phone, you succeed. You suc-ceed when you achieve your objectives. But you can't achieve your objectives unless you know exactly what they are! Use your "Call Planning and Objectives Form" before each impor-tant call.

SAVE THE SMALL TALK

Once you've determined your objective, achieve it before squandering your time with small talk. Consider beginning im-portant business calls with a quick overview of the main sub-jects you plan to cover. Reach agreement with the other person item by item. With your objectives achieved and business out of the way, you can enjoy the small talk. Business first. Then, the informal exchanges that cement our long-term business relationships.

BUILDING A PHONE WORK STATION

The physical placement of the telephone on your desk dramati-cally influences what you're able to accomplish with it. In most offices, desk phones are placed right in the midst of the clutter. When that phone rings, it reaches out and grabs your atten-tion. But as you speak, the papers you've just been working with, your stack of callback notes, and your spilling-over pile of priority projects are all sharing the same visual space with your phone. They can only distract you.

Move your phone to the side of your desk, perhaps on a credenza or low file cabinet. Immediately adjacent to the phone, keep a fresh notepad and a favored pen. This sanctuary helps shelter you from the bog-downs that occur when inbound calls catch you unprepared. The physical space works as a "mental anchor." When you turn to that place in your office, you shift into your "professional communicator" mode.

Be sure that the phone is placed so that you cannot see others in the office. If you're facing a hallway, your passing colleagues will catch your attention and break your concentration. They'll also be tempted to enter your office to drop something off or to scrawl a note. Make yourself appear uninviting and/or inaccessible when on the phone.

Telemarketing professionals, people whose daily earnings depend on their ability to persuade others, have discovered that mirrors contribute to monetary earnings. It's true. People like to do business with others who sound friendly. To increase your chances of making headway with others on the phone, project a friendly tone of voice. And the best way to sound friendly is to look friendly! No doubt about it. The shape of your mouth does influence how you sound. If you look sullen, you'll sound sullen. Smile and you will sound friendly. Place a small mirror near your phone as a reminder.

Somewhere very close to the phone, keep a rapid-access file of the people who are most likely to call you. You take some giant steps toward balancing the scale of control when you have available background material in front of you during the call.

And by all means, keep a clock in plain view. Be conscious of the time you are investing in the call. When the value received doesn't compare favorably with the time you're taking, wrap it up.

Maintain this phone station as your sanctuary. Regardless of what happens to the rest of your office, keep this one small place neat and ready for concentrated action.

MY PHONE STATION

I've assembled a very effective personal calling station in my own office. It combines the best time savers I've come across.

Furniture The tabletop at my phone station is larger than my office desk. I favor a long piece of butcher block on top of two low filing cabinets. The large surface allows me to spread out notes and past correspondence during conversations. And, of course, I need room for phone gadgets.

The chair I use rolls easily from the main desk area to my phone station. I'm comfortable in the ergonomically designed seat, and the five-leg design prevents me from tilting back (or over). During the course of a phone call, I may stay in the chair, but scoot across the room to retrieve some old files.

Paper and Pencil But not just any paper and pencil. I use photocopies of forms for note-taking, callbacks, and objective planning, all made into pads. Personally, I'm a stickler for good sharp pencils with almost-new erasers. I recommend also keeping several colored pens or pencils handy to highlight especially important details or deadlines.

Mirror Drop the notion that people can't see you when you're calling by phone. My visage (and yours) is broadcast over the wires. A glance in the mirror just before calling gives me a glimpse of the face that "other guy" is about to visualize. If I look glum in the mirror, that's just how I'm going to sound.

Answering Machine I find the machine a potent and indispensable auxiliary phone tool and use it constantly. It's best to have a private line or specific extension that reaches this "voice mailbox" when you're away from your desk. Make sure messages from you are always current. When someone reaches your machine on a Wednesday and hears you announce that it's a beautiful Monday morning, it sounds as if you don't pay much attention to your messages.

Phone   Your choices are wide open these days. But there are some features you *must* have:

Speaker phone with on-hook dialing. You pick up the receiver only after (or if) your party answers. This means that your hands will be free while you are on hold, listening to elevator music, et cetera. This single feature is a tremendous time saver. When you are placing a call to a busy manager and it takes three transfers to reach him, you needn't pick up the phone until he does.

Automatic on-hook redial. The phone will periodically redial a busy number every half minute or so. If the line is still busy, your phone detects the busy signal and "hangs up." Half a minute later, it tries again. You hear the dialing and busy signal over the speaker phone, but you never reach for the handset until you hear ringing. Meanwhile, you're attending to odds and ends or reviewing the objectives for this call and notes from recent conversations.

This is especially helpful when calling government agencies. We all know that some bureaucrats place most of their lines on hold to prevent annoying interruptions from citizens! Automatic redial will help preserve your sanity while improving your chances for getting through when a line does become available.

Auto-dial memory. Programming your frequently called numbers saves time, of course. But you can also make use of this timesaving feature by having your secretary program in your callback numbers. Callback messages in your stack should include the auto-dial codes, so you connect immediately. If you are unsuccessful in that attempt, the number is preprogrammed for a later re-try.

One of my consulting clients, Peter Rasmussen, was one of those one-man-show entrepreneurs who single-handedly established an advertising publication and personally sold over a million dollars in advertising each year. Peter accomplished an amazing amount all by himself, and one of his secrets was programming his auto-dialer when he didn't have the energy to make any more sales calls. Next morning, his prospects' data sheets were all stacked up, ready to go. He simply touched the coded auto-dial button for each one, thus moving ahead quickly without breaking momentum to look up and dial long-distance numbers.

Extra-long cords. Communicating consciously by phone is hard work! You're intently focused on the call, taking notes, listening between the lines, giving feedback. The last thing you want to do is hasten the physical drain by staying in one spot. Glued to a chair and tethered with a short phone cord, you can't help sounding somewhat sluggish.

To sound animated and lively, move around. Get your blood coursing. Be invigorated. Replace the standard short handset cord with a twenty-one-foot coiled extension. Unfettered, you can stand up and flex, fish out files, reach for a calculator, and so on. When you move about, you wake up your body, and thus, your voice. Be alert and you sound alert.

Headsets. We tend to think of phone headsets as something that only an operator would use. In fact, efficiency-minded innovators at all levels of business find that headsets allow them to accomplish more, more comfortably.

When superagent Ken Kragen is on the phone with Kenny Rogers or Lionel Richie, he's using a headset. Ken and his executive assistants wear them all day long. When putting together a major event such as the "We Are the World" recording sessions, anything that lends an extra edge of efficiency is greatly appreciated. (If you've got back problems, as Ken does, you'll also appreciate the therapeutic benefit of keeping your neck and spinal column straight throughout the day.)

Heavy phone users who spend hours with their necks crinked while cradling a phone help fill chiropractors' offices. And it can be much worse. Matt Gilbert, a telemarketing professional with ICS in Orange County, California, carries a very ugly four-inch scar near his left elbow. After months of cradling a handset with his elbow propped on a desk, Matt began to notice a persistent pain in his elbow. When he complained to his doctor, the physician knowingly asked, "Matt, do you spend lots of time on the phone?" The doctor indicated that such nerve pinching is not uncommon among heavy phone users who rest their elbows on desktops. Extensive corrective surgery was the only remedy.

Anyone who uses the phone intensively will benefit from using a headset. These devices:

- improve your efficiency by freeing your hands so you can jot notes and reach for records.
- reduce distracting background noises so that you can concentrate your full attention on the call.
- cut fatigue by improving your posture.
- brighten your voice by letting you gesticulate and move around freely.

I'm not suggesting that you harness yourself to your phone for the day. But during those periods when you've reserved blocks of time for a long series of callbacks, slip on a headset and you'll breeze ahead.

IMPROVING COMMUNICATIONS WITHIN YOUR ORGANIZATION

WHERE THE BEST IDEAS ARE

When corporations hire me for consulting projects to uncover good ideas about how to improve their telecommunications, I know just where to begin. The best ideas are already there, readily available in bountiful supply. But they're largely untapped.

The best place to begin looking for advice is within your own organization. Ask your entire staff—switchboard operators, secretaries, vice presidents—to identify the communications problems plaguing them and ask what improvements they'd suggest. Mine the great ideas your co-workers have. Dig them out. As your organization becomes more collectively phone-conscious, brainstorm!

While the complete process for conducting formal brainstorming is quite exacting, you'll easily uncover loads of valuable ideas by following these simple steps:

Raise the Phone-consciousness of Your Organization   Circulate a notice informing everyone just how much time and money you invest in telecommunications. Give them the totals from a couple of recent phone bills. They'll be shocked.

Give Specific Assignments   Don't simply ask your staff to think of ways to improve. Ask each person in the organization to write out three problems that rob him of work time while using the phone. And three suggested solutions. Set a firm time for a brainstorming session.

Let People Think   Be sure there's approximately a one-week span between the assignment memo and the brainstorm. If you leave it much longer, everyone will forget about it.

Hold a Formal Session   There are several hallmarks of a good brainstorming session:
They're short. One hour maximum.
They're led by a facilitator whose role is not to create or critique, but simply to moderate and encourage the flow of ideas.
They start with a creative warm-up. My favorite involves a boxful of unrelated items gathered from around the office: for example, a bud vase, a broken stapler handle, a calculator, and a stamp pad. Each person in the group chooses one item at random. The person who begins chooses a second item from the box and is asked to describe a relationship between the two. He or she suggests putting the two items together in a way that'll meet some need in the marketplace and make a million bucks. Once finished, this person passes one item of his choice to the next person at the table, who must now create a link between it and the item she already has. The results can be hilarious and very creative.
During one brainstorming session I conducted, the two items that ended up in a secretary's hands were a small postage scale and a vinyl page divided into several different sized pockets for photos. She thought for a moment, then described how filling the pockets with water and weighing them at timed

intervals would give you a clear reading on the rate of evaporation. The product would be called an "Evapo-Rater" and would find an active market among photographers working in tropical rain forest locations. This sounds ridiculous, but it loosened everybody up and unlocked creativity. When those juices start flowing, new—sometimes blindingly obvious—solutions to long-standing problems are the result.

They're positive. One of the facilitator's key roles is to squelch negativity. One person will say, "Well, we could cut down on missed calls by carrying cordless phones out on the factory floor." Another person immediately dampens the energy with, "Are you kidding? Do you know what that would cost?" Stamp out all such negative reactions. The facilitator's role is to say, "Every idea has some merit and our job is to modify and add to them, not criticize. Cordless phones could help. Now, let's get several more ideas going."

Look for something positive to say about every idea that's offered. Create an environment that favors the outpouring of ideas without risk of ridicule.

They're visual. I prefer to tack large sheets from a sketch pad or flipchart all over the walls. (Lesson from experience: First, be positive that your felt pens don't penetrate through the paper to the wall. I left one Citicorp boardroom with a lasting reminder of our brainstorming session.) As ideas flow out, capture them quickly. Ideas on one list will trigger someone's visual connection with a complementary idea on anther wall.

They're time-limited. The facilitator gets the best results when he begins with statements like this: "Let's focus now on ways to reduce the number of missed connections when calling our branch offices. In three minutes, let's get fifteen good ideas up on the sheet. Joseph, what's one thing you suggest?"

The ideas are culled later. First, get lots of ideas up on the walls. Thin them down later. Once all the ideas have been written out, go back and get a little bit judgmental. "Now, we've got fifteen different ideas here, all designed to cut down the switchboard load. Let's narrow it down to the five or six that can be put into action with a good chance of making a noticeable improvement right away."

They're followed up with results. After the brainstorming session, circulate a summary of the culled ideas. Let everybody continue to think about, modify, and improve on the ideas. As they're implemented, be sure that everyone in the organization knows how much time and money are being saved. Credit the brainstorm session's participants. And, of course, encourage further suggestions and improvements.

The examples of employee-initiated improvements are wide-ranging. Sometimes they are very obvious; other times quite unique. During one such session, the computer center clerks at the U.S. Senate expressed frustration because certain key specialists were hard to track down when pressing problems arose. One of the suggested solutions was to equip the handful of specialists with beepers so they could be contacted anywhere in the Senate building. The solution worked well and is now in effect. Although the beeper system might seem obvious, the problem had persisted for years and the center's management had little awareness of it.

One of the nation's most critical top-security centers is operated by the Control Data Corporation in a nondescript, unmarked building in Maryland. Its systems are accessed by remote users around the country, including the Department of Defense. The telephone center takes calls from users requesting information about several "families" of mainframe computer systems. When any one of the systems "goes down," the lines light up like Christmas trees. Since all calls come through a call-sequencing unit equipped with a tape recording, brainstorming employees suggested preparing several cassettes. When one system has problems and the staff is deluged with calls, they now simply insert an appropriate cassette. Thanks to this employee-originated idea, callers now first hear a message saying, "The KT406 System is down due to a power failure. We expect service to be restored within two hours. If your call concerns one of the other computers, please stay on the line. Otherwise, we'll continue giving our full attention to this problem to restore service as quickly as possible."

It took Michael LeBoeuf's *Greatest Management Principle in the World* to remind us of the obvious: The behavior we reward is the behavior that will be repeated. Rare is the organization that rewards and reinforces creative problem-solving behavior, so we don't see much of it. Because the phone is such a pervasive part of any organization's activity, and since its use is fraught with time-wasting inefficiencies, this is an ideal place to begin. Build a reward structure that encourages everyone in your organization to suggest improvements.

LISTENING

Most time loss during actual calls results from poor listening skills. The communication authority and Executive Director of the International Listening Association, Dr. Lyman K. Steil, has exhaustively researched communications behavior and, in particular, listening habits. He's the architect of Sperry Corporation's renowned Listening Program, and he advises every branch of the American military services.

Perhaps the most interesting of Dr. Steil's findings is that we do much more listening than anything else. We communicate during about 80 percent of our waking hours. What we do least is write; it accounts for just 9 percent of our communicating activity. Only 16 percent of our communicating time is used to read. We speak during 30 percent of the time. Listening accounts for fully 45 percent of our communicating behavior.

We were all taught to write, read, and speak. But did you *ever* get any formal training in listening, the skill you need most often? Unfortunately, our almost total lack of listening training has resulted in horrid listening skills. The average American listens at an *effective rate* of only 25 percent. Nearly half of our communication time is only a quarter as effective as it could be.

This very low rate of listening effectiveness has been documented in numerous university studies conducted since 1948. They all concur. An individual's immediate recall of the average brief message is only 50 percent. Within forty-eight hours that falls off to 25 percent. And that drop is even more pronounced when the listener has only his aural senses at work, as during a phone call.

Even if you were meeting face to face, you would forget half of what you heard immediately. But on the phone, where distractions undermine your concentration and you're deprived of visual input, the situation is worse. Think back to a recent, involved phone call. If you can recall more than a quarter of the important points two days after hanging up, you're ahead of the odds. And if your recall is that good, probably you already use many of the good listening skills outlined below.

Poor listening skills result in a hidden but pernicious problem in American business (not to mention in marriages—as attested by our divorce rates)! The problem can be dramatically reduced with training in the simple basics of listening. To ensure that you accurately hear what's being said—and what's *not* being said—while keeping yourself and the caller organized:

Prepare to Listen   It's an active process, a far cry from the popular perception that listening is simply "shutting up" and letting the information flow in. The need to prepare is exactly why inbound calls are so difficult to manage effectively. They catch us off guard, unprepared.

Turn Away From Your Other Work   Set up a call station that allows you to focus on the call alone; not the other projects on your desk. Turn your attention and vision away from all distractions.

Consciously Keep an Open Mind   When you're not in control of the time you spend on a call, it's easy to get impatient. You start feeling that you pretty well understand the caller's point before it's even made.

Let the Other Person Speak Without Interruption   Even on inbound calls you can be in control. Realize that the best way to get the most information, most quickly, is to let the speaker talk without interruption. When the caller is wandering about, keep her on track by exercising outlining skills.

"Janet, I want to be sure I'm sticking with you. Am I correct in thinking that you have three major concerns about this plan?"

Provide Oral Feedback   While you don't want to interrupt the speaker, you do want to let her know that you are intently focused on the message. It's helpful to offer low-level messages that encourage the speaker.

"I see . . . Uh-huh . . . Interesting! . . . Tell me more . . . Go on . . . And then what happened?"

Adopt the Same Physical Posture You'd Use if the Caller Were There in Front of You   The science of kinesics, usually called "body language," draws a major distinction between "open" and "closed" postures. If you want to show the other person that you do want to hear, that you're open to what she is saying, you use the "open" posture. Uncross your limbs and keep your posture erect and attentive. The "closed" posture communicates exactly the opposite. If the caller were right there in front of you, you'd never slouch down in the chair, fiddle with a paperclip, and look bored. But don't we do that all the time on the phone? You help yourself to listen—and that results in saved time—when you maintain an erect, attentive posture. We'll discuss body language extensively in the "Power Talking" chapter.

Take Notes During Every Call   Preferably, use an outlining guide that you create to accurately record call details. One excellent technique is to draw a vertical line down the middle of your note page. Label one side "Facts/Statements" and the other "Impressions/Reactions." You're most attentive when several senses are involved. As you record the speaker's messages, you keep yourself actively involved by also noting your feelings about them. Taking notes ensures that your motor reflexes and visual senses, as well as your aural senses, are active. Be sure to retain these message forms. In these litigious times, you never know when you'll be glad to have a formal written record of previous conversations.

Repeat and Verify All Key Facts   This is the vital "feedback loop" that makes communication much more accurate and effective. You pay the other person a great compliment when you say something like:

> "Your business is very important to me and I want to be absolutely sure that I understand you clearly. I jotted some notes as you were explaining the situation. Let me verify with you that I've gotten it all accurately . . . ."

It's very important that you take personal responsibility for getting the message right. Be certain that you don't say anything that might be incorrectly interpreted. You don't want to sound as if you're implying:

> "*You* can be pretty confusing and downright muddled. Since you're hard to understand anyway, you'd better repeat that for me."

The biggest problem voiced by telephone professionals can be solved by simply taking charge of the situation. Commitment to streamlining your business day through creative thought and determined organizational efforts is the key. If the suggestions outlined in this chapter seem as if they require too much time, think of them as that ounce of prevention that is worth a pound of cure. The time you'll save will amaze you. And you won't cringe next time the phone rings, put off calling that government agency, or worse yet, stall another day avoiding someone you said you'd call a week ago. You'll be in control!

4

POWER TALKING: PROJECT MORE AUTHORITY WITH YOUR VOICE AND WORDS

Secretary: "Mr. Basteau, Mark Draper is down in the lobby for you."

Executive: "Who? Is that the guy who thinks my name is 'bay-stew'?"

Secretary: "That's him. But don't feel bad. When he phones here he always calls me 'Miss Efficiency' just before he cuts me off. And for him, three words a minute is really zooming."

Executive: "Sounds like bad news to me. Show him in, but buzz me in fifteen minutes and tell me I have to rush to a board meeting. Let's get him out of here. I don't want to waste much time with him."

Businesspeople looking for an edge study fashion implications, body language, meeting-leader strategies, and power-writing phrases. They track which drinks are in vogue, how to negotiate, and just about everything else they think will get them maximum results from their business encounters.

All of these things do affect interpersonal dynamics and are important for face-to-face meetings. Yet, in reality, most business today starts with phone connections. Our first impressions come from the initial contact. More often than not, that's a phone call.

Consider the scenario of a career change or job search. Most people focus tremendous attention on preparing a beautiful résumé and professional cover letter. But the truth is, nothing in your whole search is as important as the impression you make on your first phone call. Recruiters and employers say that they carefully evaluate résumés and exhaustively research your background. But the reality is that much of the basic hiring decision is made in the first few minutes. Résumés and other information simply reinforce gut-level first reactions.

The world's largest ad agency, Young & Rubicam, and the world's second largest, Dentsu, have formed a joint venture in Los Angeles. Bill Lyddan is the director of client services, and interviews candidates for key positions right up to the senior VP level. Bill tells it like it is:

> "I believe you can tell exactly what a person is like on the phone. His phone manner—language, assertiveness, tone of voice—accurately reflect what he's really like. Within five minutes, I'm 75 percent sure if a candidate will fit here."

IT'S MORE *HOW* YOU SAY IT THAN WHAT YOU SAY

We're usually very concerned about saying "the right things." But *what* you say is far less important than *how* you say it. Dr. Albert Mehrabian of UCLA's psychology department has quantitatively determined how people communicate their feelings when conversing. Surprise! Only 7 percent of the feeling communicated in a spoken message is conveyed by the words themselves. Thirty-eight percent comes from *how* we speak— the tone, volume, inflection, et cetera. A whopping 55 percent of meaning is conveyed nonverbally with body language.

An irate customer barges into the customer service department. Carl Portnoy looks up from his untidy desk. He sees the angry man and leans back in his chair, arms crossed. Tilting back, Carl puts one foot up on a pulled-out drawer. His gaze shifts to the clock on his desk and he takes on a pained expression. In a loud, hurried, but completely monotone drone, he says: "Tell me all about it. I'll see what I can do."

An irate customer barges into the customer service department. Carl Portnoy looks up from his tidy desk. Seeing the unhappy man, Carl stands and approaches him. Extending a hand, he directs the customer toward a comfortable chair and sits beside him. Carl reaches for a clean pad of paper and pen. He leans slightly toward the customer, makes a strong visual connection and smiles. His reassuring, sympathetic facial expression conveys a sense of, "It's all right. I'll listen and help." In a forthright voice, Carl says, "Tell *me* about it. (slight pause) *I'll* see what I *can* do."

Same words. Totally different message.

VOICE VARIABLES

Just as your selection of words and your choice of body postures profoundly influence how your message is "heard," so does your voice. How you sound isn't an inescapable result of cultural factors, upbringing, and physical characteristics. Dump the notion that you're stuck with the way you sound right now. Your voice is a matter of *choice*.

A close friend of mine grew up in the Bronx. He sounds like it. He is constantly putting himself down because he "don't soun' so good." But how he sounds—or how *you* sound—is a matter of choice. My friend can, next week, enroll in a speech class or take English in night school—if he chooses to. We can all shape the images we project to the world.

Dr. Morton Cooper is perhaps America's best-known voice specialist. He has trained celebrities from Henry Fonda and Joan Rivers to O. J. Simpson and Diahann Carroll. Dr.

Cooper is convinced that a "magic voice" is the one trait shared by almost all who achieve greatness. He stresses the importance of projecting a positive "voice image." His book *Change Your Voice, Change Your Life* is highly recommended for its discussion of the therapeutic aspects of voice improvement. We're concerned here not so much with therapy as with the immediate application of simple techniques that will change your ability to really come across during your very next phone call.

While teaching public seminars around the country, I always use a revealing exercise to demonstrate the importance of voice variables. I ask a class filled with strangers in a darkened meeting room to cover their eyes and speak to each other for fifteen seconds. That's about three sentences. Then, without forewarning, I ask each participant to select only four adjectives (from a list of thirty) that describe the person they've just heard but can't see.

Fifteen seconds doesn't seem like a long enough time to form judgments about a stranger. But try it yourself. You don't need any blindfold. Just pause fifteen seconds into your next phone conversation with a stranger. Ask yourself to describe the other person and you'll have no trouble coming up with a complete profile. You'll know if that person is confident, intelligent, a clear thinker, honest, friendly . . . or not. If the person you're speaking with stopped to perform this same exercise, he'd be able to quickly—and accurately—size you up after just a few seconds. In fact, that's exactly what we all do.

What people talk *about* in the exercise is totally inconsequential. Sometimes I suggest that they describe what happened en route to the seminar room; sometimes I ask them to explain why they like their favorite ice cream flavor; sometimes I tell them to describe their bosses. The results are always the same, regardless of the subject discussed.

After many rooms full of blindfolded strangers, there are three things of which I'm certain:

We form abundant impressions of others very quickly—in seconds—even though we have only their voices to evaluate. Ninety percent of the people who go through this exercise wish they weren't limited to just four adjectives. Rather than saying, "How do you expect me to describe this stranger after only fifteen seconds?", their primary concern is compressing their profuse observations into just four words.

Our impressions aren't capricious guesses; they're based on specific, objective criteria. The hardest—and most revealing—part of this exercise is figuring out exactly why each adjective was chosen. At first, nearly everyone says, "Oh, I don't know, she just *seemed* that way to me." When pressed, there's always a very good reason behind the choices.

> "I rated her as cheerful because she has a lot of variation in her tone of voice."
>
> "He seemed intelligent because I noticed that he used two unusual and well-chosen words."
>
> "I checked her as conscientious because I noticed that she was very careful with her enunciation."
>
> "I marked him as confident because he started talking right away without hesitating, and he also spoke strongly, but not too loudly."
>
> "He struck me as shy and reserved because I had to strain to hear what he was saying."

All of the factors that contribute to those impressions are alterable. Your volume, word choice, rate of speech, timing, enunciation, tone, et cetera, are all within your control. If you want to project an image that differs from the impressions you're currently giving people, *you can.*

DEVELOPING RAPPORT

Careful! Don't head off to polish your language and voice so that you match some academician's view of the "right" way to sound. At the bottom line, true communication depends not just on clear pronunciation, careful choice of words, and a smiling face. It stems from a feeling of rapport. Actively developing rapport is one of the keys to conscious contact.

You call people to communicate with them. And that's done on two levels. Yes, there are facts and information to exchange. But first, the doors of rapport have to open. Rapport can be loosely defined as a feeling of "sameness." When we feel rapport with others, the channels are open; we're "on the same wavelength"; we feel we could become friends. There are lots of direct, explicit techniques for developing rapport. They include:

- using the other person's name during the conversation (in moderation).
- mentioning acquaintances by name, or making reference to mutual experiences or backgrounds.
- asking questions about the other person's viewpoint. This demonstrates that you're not self-centered; that you are interested in understanding his position.
- stating openly that your aims are the same; that you both share common goals and that this conversation is an opportunity to reach mutual satisfaction.

Without rapport, we don't fully communicate; both parties are less likely to achieve their objectives. And rapport certainly plays a major role in gaining a feeling of satisfaction about the call. Some of the most effective rapport-developing techniques are very subtle.

It's important to note that people think—and express themselves—in three main ways. A communicator's thoughts will be represented internally by either:

- visual images he will generate,
- feelings he will have, or
- his silently "talking" to himself and "hearing words."

These three systems may be referred to as visual, kinesthetic, and auditory. Throughout any communication exchange, an individual switches among systems frequently. But, generally, one predominates.

If the person you speak with says,

"As I *look* at this, I *see* lots of confusion. Perhaps you can *shed some light* on a few points,"

and you want to heighten your chances of being understood clearly and without resistance, you'll respond,

"Yes, I can *see* how confusing this must *appear*. Let's *look* at it from another angle and I'll *see* if I can create a *clearer picture*."

You wouldn't say,

"It *sounds* like you haven't *heard* what I'm *talking* about. *Listen* to it this way."

You two would be on different channels!

If you want to establish rapport, it's useful to match the representational systems others use. You do this by listening carefully and then "packaging" what you want to express before it travels from your mind to your mouth to their ears. Target their representational systems and your statements will be more readily disgested. You'll be building rapport.

A person who uses a lot of action-packed adverbs and colorful descriptions is likely to tire of listening to a dull, bare-essentials speaker. Likewise, the less imaginative speaker will feel overwhelmed by—or even defensive toward—his flamboyant-tongued counterpart.

You should also be attentive to the more obvious aspects of the other person's speech patterns. If you speak loudly at 212 words per minute, and the stranger you call speaks softly at 140, you're not on the same wavelength. The other person will not feel comfortable if you sound markedly different.

True communication is getting the response you seek. If you aren't getting the response you want, change, adapt, *model* your behavior after those with whom you wish to communicate. Don't fight or challenge. One who wishes to communicate superbly practices these three techniques:

1. She knows what the desired results of the communication are.
2. She has the flexibility to quickly adapt to the other party's communication patterns, including her choice of words, volume, speaking rate, and so forth.
3. And finally, she has the perspicacity to recognize when desired results start to take form.

The need to establish rapport by mirroring the other person's communication patterns is particularly pronounced when calling between distinct regions. A New Yorker calling Oklahoma or Arkansas faces a real challenge! Put all of these voice variables to work and you'll open the door of rapport more quickly and communicate objective facts more clearly.

SPEAKING RATE

The average American speaks at about 150 words per minute. But that figure gives you no help at all in deciding how rapidly you should speak to any particular individual on the phone. If you're calling your broker on Wall Street during a rally, you'd better crank it up. If you've reached Grandpa at his home outside Baton Rouge at 2:30 Sunday afternoon . . . whoa!

We can effectively transmit and receive facts only when we're "in tune" with each other. One of the best ways to subtly create rapport is with adjustments in speaking rate. The key is to mirror the other person's natural rate of speech.

I was at home, relaxing after dinner. The beef was perfectly broiled, the wine's bouquet just right. The phone rang and the siege began:

"GoodEvening,Mr.Walther. We'vegotaVERYspecial offeravailableONLYto newsubscriberswho likeyou, Mr.Walther,live andworkhereinthe SouthernCalifornia area. Now,Mr.Walther,thisISa no-risk offer andI'vebeen authorized bymysupervisor togiveyoutheSPECIALtwo-month GetAcquainted—"

CLICK! Too fast for me.

And on the other hand, how successful would I be calling my agent under these circumstances:

The secretary is late again, Richard has one line on hold, is negotiating with a major publisher on Wayne Dyers's next book, owes a callback to Simon and Schuster Video, and is having a very hectic morning.

> "Hi, there, Richard. How ya doin? . . . What about those Mets? . . . Well, hang on a minute, Richard. . . . Ah, well. Let's see. . . I wanted ta chat about a few things here, ah . . . Now, ah, I bin thinkin . . ."

Good bye, Richard! Not that he'd hang up. He would stay on the line, but his mind would be gone. First, he'd roll his eyes and feel resentful that I was robbing him of precious minutes. Then, he'd start figuring how to get me out of his hair.

The first step in getting the other guy's attention is to be sure that you adjust your speaking rate to his. This immediately works in favor of developing rapport, and it also ensures that you'll be speaking at a rate that's comfortable for him.

Remember, talk too quickly and you're immediately perceived as one of those "fast-talkers." If you're lucky, the other person will just feel a bit uncomfortable. More likely, you'll be putting the other person off. The guard goes up. "What is he trying to slip past me?"

Dr. Norman Miller, a psychology professor at the University of Southern California, has researched the effects of speaking rate on perceptions of intelligence and credibility. To different audiences he played recordings of identical manuscripts on various subjects, all read by the same speaker, but at different rates. He found that the faster versions were consistently rated as more credible. What's more, audiences that heard the faster versions gave the speaker higher ratings for being knowledgeable and intelligent!

I don't recommend getting carried away with the results of this research. Don't barrel ahead in an attempt to foster an extremely erudite image by speaking superfast. But if you're to err one way or the other, it's safest to speak just a bit more rapidly than the other person. Speak too slowly and you lose the other party's attention. Speak much too rapidly and you destroy rapport. The most effective course: adjust your speaking rate to the other person's, and perhaps crank it up a notch to reinforce impressions of intelligence.

VOLUME

Your volume level can build or destroy rapport. It can also aid or hinder the communication of information on the objective level. If the other party is soft-spoken, and you come across with a booming voice, you'll probably be perceived as overbearing. There goes rapport. If you speak softly, this may be interpreted as an indication that you aren't all that sure of what you're saying.

Again, adjust your volume to the other person's volume. Speak just a little more loudly and you project confidence.

One important exception: If the person you speak with is emotionally charged, don't match his or her hollering. Soothe and calm the caller by subtly de-escalating the emotions with your measured volume.

Developing rapport with voice variables isn't difficult. It's simply making conscious contact. If you consciously aim to make contact clear and meaningful, your instincts will handle the adjustments.

DICTION

Diction encompasses both word choice and manner of speaking, or enunciation. Diction is the primary ingredient listeners use in sizing us up. On the basis of diction, we're quickly judged as to our intelligence, education, upbringing, even ethnicity. What an opportunity to create impressions!

Imprecise or improper words, sloppily uttered or mispronounced, leave us indelibly branded. If your first sentence is,

"I'm callin' about the stuff in your ad, you know, like the job positions . . ."

you have little chance of recovering later in the conversation.

The best way to assess the quality of your diction is to hear yourself. There's just no substitute for a tape recorder. To get an accurate reading of how the world hears you, place a small tape recorder on your desk during the course of a regular workday. If possible, use the voice-activated type. This feature lets you leave the recorder on at all times. It begins recording as soon as you begin speaking, and then shuts down during periods of silence. Pay particular attention to how you sound during telephone conversations.

As you listen to and review these tapes, you will notice aspects of your own pronunciation and word choice that you don't like. Hearing them yourself, deciding you don't like them, and becoming attuned to the shortfalls is far more effective and practical than having some speech teacher tell you the way you ought to sound.

Most diction problems are not the result of incorrect pronunciation; they're simply due to careless habits. Going to a school, hiring a speech tutor, and reading dictionaries is helpful but probably not necessary. The answer to improving diction is very simple—conscious contact. Most of us can speak more clearly without outside help. Once aware of our sloppiness, we do the job ourselves. Of course, the taping process should continue as a periodic self-check.

When we deal with people face-to-face, they assess our physical stature, wardrobe, handshake, the amount of moisture on our upper lips, how evenly we trim our fingernails—the works. By phone, they go through the same assessing process, but work from fewer and far more limited cues. A single slip or mispronunciation, one wrong word choice, and the judgmental process begins; we're pigeonholed.

BODY TALK

Your voice is like a window that lets the other person see you. If you have a bored posture, you sound bored and you're perceived as bored. Are you alert, erect, eager? You'll sound that way, and project that image, too.

See for yourself. Midway through your next call, draw the other person's face and fill in the shape of the mouth as he/she speaks. It will take only a few words before you know how it looks. People who are smiling sound like they are. Glum? Easily detected from voice tone.

If you closed off the bell-shaped opening of a bugle, you'd change the sound altogether. Your vocal cords, throat, and mouth form your personal instrument. You can just as easily shape its sound by changing the shape of your mouth.

Now picture Carl Portnoy from the beginning of this chapter answering the phone rather than facing the customer at his desk. Don't exactly the same impressions apply? If he tilts back in his chair and looks bored, that's precisely how he comes across on the phone. His closed posture conveys a clear message: "I'm not interested in what you're saying. You are foreign to me and I'm protecting myself from your influence. Don't for a minute think we're seeing eye-to-eye. I don't want your problems to take up my time. I wish you hadn't called."

When Carl gets a complaint call, his first action is the most critical. More important than what he *says* is what he *does*. If he adopts the open posture, ready to listen, two things happen:

He sends a clear signal to the caller. The other person literally "hears" his body posture. Right now, lean back in your chair, cross your arms and legs. Slump down and put your feet up. Say, "I'm concerned about this and I want to hear all about what happened."

Now, sit forward. Take a deep breath. Get a pen and paper ready. Uncross your arms and legs and relax your hands. Again, say "I'm concerned about this and I want to hear all about what happened." You do sound different. The message in your open posture is also clear: "I want to hear you and I'm listening. Your thoughts are important to me. I'm open to what you are saying."

The difference may be barely discernible to your conscious ear, but your more perceptive "inner ear" gets the signal. Science has only begun to scratch the surface of understanding how thoroughly and deeply we register our perceptions of each other. Our subconscious "ears" are far more attuned to voice inflections, tone variations, and the "how" of our speech than we realize.

He sends himself a clear signal. Focusing on body posture and making a physical adjustment because you want to sound better sends a feedback signal to yourself. You're saying, "I choose to consciously manage my reactions." That's what puts you in control.

I recently became involved in an extended and very frustrating battle with the IRS. They charged me with having failed to report $600 in income three years earlier from a small seminar company in Colorado. In fact, the $600 entry was clearly included on my return, along with the 1099 form. The affair took on battle proportions. Eventually, I received a notice from the IRS telling me that my property would be seized if I didn't clear up the matter. I had been doing my darndest to clear the matter up for months.

I panicked upon realizing that I was three days short of the appeal deadline. One of the notices indicated that if I did not lodge an appeal with the Federal Tax Court by the deadline, there would be no chance for any future appeal. I couldn't believe this was all happening over such an obvious IRS oversight concerning a very minor item. I certainly did not want the "big computer" to have my name flagged as a tax dodger.

I caught a glance of myself in the mirror while talking with a faceless clerk in the Fresno Regional Center. There I was, hunched forward, legs crossed, actually extending my finger in an accusatory gesture. My body was literally poised to lunge forward and grasp the IRS by its bureaucratic neck. Not only did I feel annoyed, I was getting nowhere.

Later that same day, I received a call from yet another IRS office. A friendly, apologetic young woman told me that the IRS had made a terrible mistake. She was unaware of the telephone battles I'd been waging all day. She was simply calling with good news.

As she closed the call, miraculously pronouncing that "the case is closed," I once again looked at myself in that mirror. I appeared alert, receptive, and attentive and had a much more relaxed facial expression. Rather than pointing and lunging, I was quietly taking notes on all that she'd said. I felt like hugging this person who had brought an end to my troubles. And my body posture showed how relieved I felt.

With a day full of tense confrontations and hostile, unproductive phone battles, this one single call had put an end to my worries. As I reflected on the calls of the day, I felt sure that I would not only have made more progress, but also would have felt much better had I taken body posture inventory before and during the earlier IRS calls. Would I have reached resolution sooner? I know I would have felt better even if the outcome had been unchanged. And my improved disposition just may have helped me make headway. Check your own posture and facial expression next time you're getting nowhere on the phone.

TONE

Though "tone" is a hard quality to nail down, most people first name it as the main tool they use to assess other people's voices. Tone of voice is influenced by both inner attitudes and physical postures. People who are bored sound that way. Positive-thinking go-getters come across that way. What people usually call "tone" is actually the sum of speaking rate, volume, inflection, choice of words—and posture.

The emotional quality of voice tone dramatically influences a call's outcome. Consider a female executive calling a male colleague. The "mothering" tone of voice that soothes her children at home won't get much cooperation at work. She'll be seen as soft. A harsh, authoritative tone will brand her as a "pushy broad" and will drive others away. A warm but assertive tone lets her colleague know that she means business and intends to accomplish her objectives in a friendly way.

WHAT YOUR WORD CHOICE SAYS ABOUT YOU

Just as your voice variables—your tone, inflection, volume, and diction—influence the way others perceive you, your word choice is critical in shaping your phone image.

Cheryl: "Let's see, I'm not really too sure about that. I guess I'll have to go track this down in another department. I'll try to call you later. Uh, when would be a good time?"

Charlene: "I don't have an immediate answer to that question. I'll be glad to verify your payment with Accounting. I will reach you this afternoon. Is one-thirty convenient, or do you prefer four o'clock?"

Who sounds more like someone you'll respect, like, and want to work with? Although both Cheryl and Charlene were answering the same question, Charlene chose words promising definite action. Cheryl hedged and ended up promising no action at all.

CHOOSING POSITIVE, ACTIVE WORDS

There are two great reasons for speaking in positives: First, people understand what you have to say more readily when it's stated positively. In fact, Johns Hopkins psychologist Dr. Herbert Clark quantitatively demonstrated that, on average, a person understands positively worded statements one third more quickly that those with negative phrases.

The second, more powerful reason, is that positive, active words and statements form exactly the kind of "gets things done" image that does help get things done. To be perceived as a person who has definite answers, knows where you're going, and has authority, speak that way! Cleanse your vocabulary. Purge words and phrases like:

"I can't"   Negative! Sure, you can't schedule delivery until Friday. Say, "I *can* schedule this delivery for Friday." The facts are exactly the same, except that the statement is more readily understood, and you're seen as eager to help instead of obstruct.

"I'll try"   When you say "I'll try," you're saying one of two things:

1. I really want to accomplish this and will give it my best, but I can't promise what will happen. Or,
2. I really don't want to do what you're asking and probably won't. But I'll mollify you now by leading you to think that I may give it some effort.

If the former is true, say it. It will come across much more honestly and forthrightly and instill more confidence in your listener than "I'll try."

If the latter is true, you're still much better off saying what you mean. "No, I won't thoroughly read the report this evening. What I *will* do is scan the table of contents and start thinking about it. I will commit to a complete review by next Wednesday." And if the truth is that you do intend to accomplish a specific objective, speak positively. Let your language convey your confidence that you'll achieve your objectives.

If something's impossible, you probably know it already. You and the person you're talking with are both better off if you avoid wishy-washy, hedging words. If it can't be done, say so now, during the call.

"Have to"   This sounds like a burden. "I'll *have to* check with James" just doesn't compare well with "I'll be *glad to* check with James."

"I'll be honest with you. . . ."   As opposed to how you've been up until now? This phrase seems to indicate that you're usually *not* honest, but in this particular instance you'll make an exception. To a lesser extent, the commonly used word, "frankly" has the same effect. Have you been less than frank until now? If you want the listener to know you're being honest say "The truth is . . ."

"I'm really not too sure."   Of course you're sure. You're sure that you don't know. Say, "I don't have that information now. I'll be glad to get a definite answer and call you back with verification."

"I'd hate to . . ." Rather than taking the negative approach and saying you'd *hate* to give a *wrong* answer, put the shoe on your other foot: "I *want* to be sure you get an *accurate* answer." You're going to track down reliable information in either case. Do it positively!

"I was going to say . . ." Have you ever heard someone say, "I was gonna say, but I won't?" Of course not! We say what we were going to say anyway, so why not just say it? That prefatory "I was gonna say" is just a qualifier. You sound as if you're unsure of your statement's validity and want to precede it with a qualifier. This devalues your thought.

"When will that be ready?" Get in the driver's seat! Taking a positive, active, assertive role means that you focus on what you need and then poll others, adjusting where necessary. Instead of asking, "When will that report be ready?" say, "I'd like to have that report on Wednesday morning. Is that any problem for you?"

"I would think . . ." You *would*? If what? Don't use indefinite, conditional phrases. State affirmatively, "I believe . . ."

"May I ask your name?" Meek, meek, meek! You don't need permission to ask another person's name, do you? "What is your name, please?"

"Can I interrupt you for a minute?" You already have! First, if you feel confident reading the other person's mood, determine if this is a good time to raise your point. If it is, and your point is valid, go! Or, ask, "Jane, I know you're busy, but may we talk briefly about the Hambly project?"

"Can I ask you a question?" You already have! If the question is important enough to raise, you don't need permission to ask it. If there's doubt in your mind, save the question for later when it's your turn to clarify.

"I'll have to ask someone about that."   Who are you? *No one?* Rather than saying, "I have no idea about that; I'll have to ask someone," say, "My expertise is in A and your question concerns B. I'll be glad to contact our B specialist and get the answer for you."

"Hang on a minute while I get something to write with."   You shouldn't even pick up the phone unless you've got pen and paper ready. This phrase clearly says, "I didn't have the minimal foresight to prepare for our conversation. My work space isn't orderly enough for me to reach out and find a pencil, so waste a precious moment while I rummage around looking for one."

"Can you spell your name for me?"   What an insult! Are you implying that I may not yet have nailed down the correct spelling of my own name? The direct answer to this literal question would be, "Yes, I believe I can." Say precisely what you mean: "Please spell that for me."

"They just won't do it."   People are always talking about what others *won't* do. "Those salesmen just won't turn their reports in on time." Rather than making judgments and predicting the future, stick with the facts. "They haven't yet done it." Better yet, take responsibility. "I haven't yet gotten the salesmen's cooperation."

"If I can find out. . . ."   Project the expectation that you *will* be successful. Say instead, "When I confirm . . ."

"I'm only the . . ."   Why belittle yourself or your position? Rather than saying, "I can't answer that, I'm just the operator . . ." say "I am the operator and I'll be glad to connect you with the department best able to help you with this question." The words "only" or "just" imply inadequacy and inferiority.

WHO'S BENJAMIN WHORF AND WHAT DID HE SAY?

Most people would readily agree that we sound the way we feel. What few people realize, even though it has been proven by some prominent academicians, is that we don't just sound like we feel, we also think the way we sound.

Benjamin Whorf studied language and behavior under Yale's Professor Edward Sapir in the early twentieth century. They mostly studied American Indian languages, the Hopi tongue, in particular. They discovered that language structures actually condition the way people think. The organization of the universe as embodied in the language a person or culture uses may act as the determining factor in shaping habits of perception and thought.

What bearing does the Hopi language have on us today? Plenty! The Whorfian Hypothesis is complex and far-reaching and has important cultural implications. But on a strictly personal level the impact is clear: You think, behave, and believe the way you speak. If you say,

> "I'll *try* to call you *sometime* later. *If* we *could* chat some more, *would* that be okay?"

you might as well give up! Talk like that and it's clear that you don't really expect that the conversation will take place, and you act accordingly.

To ensure the conversation *does* take place, say,

> "I *will reach you* later in the week and we'll talk further. Is two-thirty Thursday convenient, or is first thing Friday better for you?"

Speak with the expectation of success and you propel yourself toward success.

THE IMPORTANCE OF BEING CONCISE

Chatting with friends is one thing. Communicating useful information in business is quite another. Boil it down! Get to the meat of your message and say it once. People who speak in long, convoluted sentences impress us as muddled thinkers. To be perceived as a sharp thinker, get to the point. No complaint is more common in telephone communications.

Back to my survey of telephone professionals: the two most revealing questions are:

1. What one piece of advice would you give those who call from inside your office?
2. What one piece of advice would you give those who call from outside your office?

The leading answer by far to both questions is the same: "Get to the point!"

THE TRUTH

The truth can work so well in business—and life. It's a wonder we don't use it more often. Let's all just stop avoiding it. Pervasive phrases like,

"He's just stepped away from his desk."
"Who's calling? I'll see if she's in."
and, "He's in a meeting."

are worn out.

Even when you *are* in a meeting, that phrase has little impact, except quite possibly to raise the suspicion that you're avoiding the call. While on hold, your caller probably visualizes you waving your hand to your secretary, signaling that you don't want to talk. (Once in a while, a weak-fingered secretary fails to push the hold button firmly enough and you hear the other person saying, "I don't want to talk to *her.* Say I'm in a meeting.")

Using more precise language won't compromise your privacy. It will make the "in a meeting" phrase more believable. And it makes sense to get the vital call details now rather than just jotting a number on a "While You Were Out" pad. Make it easy for listeners to believe you. Purge such suspicious phrases as:

"She's in a meeting."   "Mr. Gray, Debra is in the conference room with several of our managers. She and I will talk soon after the meeting breaks. I'll be glad to help you get connected if you'll tell me a little about your call. I may be able to help you quickly myself."

"He's not in right now. May I take a message?"   "Mr. Rollins will be in the office later this afternoon. I will be sure that he gets your message as soon as he returns. If he needs to speak with you, will you be available between three and four P.M.?"

"I'll see if she's in."   "Rosemarie is committed to a writing project at the moment. She's asked me to interrupt only in emergencies, but I'll be glad to schedule a callback right after lunch."

*   *   *

Secretary: "Mr. Basteau, I have a Mark Draper holding for you."

Executive: "Who? That name rings a bell. Wasn't he that uneducated wimp I wasted a half hour with a couple of months back?"

Secretary: "Same name, but it couldn't be the same guy. This Mark Draper sounds like a very intelligent, confident man. He's polite and gets right to the point. He said he has a way to reduce our office copier costs by twenty-five to thirty percent. He sounds like he knows what he's talking about."

Executive: "Well, that could be worth my while. I'll pick it up."

5

PHONE RELATIONS: ELEVATE YOUR ORGANIZATION'S PUBLIC IMAGE

EXCELLENCE EXPRESS

I've found two celebrated companies in America that are consistently superb with their phone relations. They both have "Express" in the company name. I wonder if that has anything to do with it.

AMERICAN EXPRESS

They do everything right. I'm a heavy user of AMEX, having personal and corporate credit cards for myself and my employees. We also accept American Express cards when filling orders for tapes or books, so we deal with the merchant division as well as the consumer credit division. They don't employ any fancy innovations that I've noticed, they just concentrate on the basics. They always answer right away. You get a knowledgeable person, not recorded elevator music or a receptionist. When they say they'll call you back, they do! The computer is never down. The person who takes your call is always well trained. This organization is just plain good, and they no doubt invest in their people to make sure they stay that way.

I recently called Cardholder Services when I had a dispute with a merchant concerning a computer I had purchased with my AMEX card. The first AMEX person I spoke with handled the entire transaction. I was not transferred at all. An empathetic woman asked me intelligent questions and gave me audible feedback as I spoke ("I see . . . And then what happened? . . . Uh-huh . . . I understand . . ."). After going through the whole story with names, dates, and details, this woman told me that she didn't handle my account. "All gold cardholders are serviced from the Florida office—"

I felt myself tense up and began to ask for the number of that office.

"—but I've entered a record in my terminal, here. I'll be glad to send a copy of the complete file to Florida for you."

"What do you need from me?"

"Nothing at all. I've made a complete record and you may simply deduct the $2138.55 from your next payment. Within sixty days, we'll let you know the outcome of our investigation. Either we'll tell you that we've resolved the issue with the vendor, or you're entitled to keep the credit."

I couldn't believe it was this easy. What had she written, I asked? The woman read back her complete record (it took about two and a half minutes in all) and it was perfect! She even had everything spelled correctly.

No wonder they're successful at American Express. And what company couldn't do as well if it decided to?

FEDERAL EXPRESS

Another example of a prominent national company with superb phone relations is Federal Express. Again, their superiority stems from their employees' conscientious mastery of the basics.

A call to their 800 number gets an almost immediate answer. The rep introduces himself by name and asks for your account number. He then immediately verifies key parts of your record. "Is this George I'm speaking with?" . . . "Will this pickup be at your regular address, 3004 Pacific Avenue?"

Throughout the conversation the rep uses the customer's name. "And, George, what is the destination zip code for this package?" Any special situations, such as international shipments, are handled by the same professional who answers the phone. If a transfer is necessary, it always begins with the original rep introducing you to the new person and explaining the situation.

Besides giving the strong impression that they are "on top of it" and will perform professionally, they do! Federal Express does, absolutely, positively, always pick up the package when they say they will, and they always get it to its destination on time.

THE BASICS GET YOU ON THE EXCELLENCE EXPRESS

Do you want to get your organization on the Excellence Express? For starters, practice *conscious contact* basics.

Answer phones within two or three rings. If this is not possible, you need to make some changes. Increase your switchboard staff. Install Centrex service or direct lines so that callers can reach appropriate extensions without burdening the switchboard.

Focus on the callers. Provide your phone personnel with comfortable, quiet workplaces free from distractions and background noises. Clattering typewriters and cacophonous conversations sabotage your efforts to project a positive image.

Make call handling a top priority. Don't expect people to concentrate their energies promoting a positive image for your organization and then ask them to simultaneously handle typing, mail sorting, greeting visitors, and so on.

Be sure that everyone in your organization greets callers in a friendly, courteous way. The ideal answer includes three components:

1. Answer with a friendly, smiling greeting. Something simple like, "Good morning!"
2. Identify the person and the organization. "You've reached Federal Express. This is Henry McCarthy."

3. State your willingness to move ahead. "How may I help you today?"

This may sound like nit-picking, but the proper question is not "Can I help you?" Who knows? Our aim is not to determine if you are capable of helping me. I just want to know that you are ready to dive right in! "How may I help you?" gets down to specifics. Let's presume that you are able to and want to help me. The real next-step question is, "In what way may I be of assistance?"

Be sure your people are trained to communicate clearly. This begins by checking to see who's on the phones right now. My home mortgage is with American Savings & Loan. For some reason, they have staffed their switchboard with an operator whose English is not clear. Her accent always leaves me with the impression that I've reached "Omega Savings." Start with clear communicators and then train them to be even better.

Don't put your callers on hold indefinitely. When you must ask callers to hold, ask them and offer a choice. "That information is filed in another room. Do you prefer to hold for two or three minutes now while I get it, or would it be more convenient for me to call you back?" Then when your callers are on hold, check back frequently. Everyone appreciates a little reassurance while they are in (as George Carlin puts it) purgatory. "Mr. Walther, I haven't forgotten you. I'll have that information in a minute." And when returning to the call, begin by thanking the caller for holding.

Confirm all transfers. If a customer walked in your front door and wanted help with a customer service problem, you would not allow the receptionist to say, "See that hallway? Go down there about fifty feet and turn left. The third door on your right is Customer Service. I'm not sure anyone's available to help right now, but if you stand around for a while, someone will probably notice you."

But isn't that exactly what a "blind transfer" does? The best way of transferring calls does take a few extra seconds. But you're not spending time, you're investing it. The long-term return from a customer base that always perceives you as a professional, and the immediate return of saving time by letting your personnel be prepared for their calls represent huge returns on those invested seconds. An ideal transfer goes like this:

Receptionist: "Good morning, American Binder Supply. This is Susan, how may I help you?"

Caller: "My name's Jesse Williams and I just received my binders, but they're the wrong color! I need them redone, fast."

Receptionist: "I'm sorry to hear there's a problem, Mr. Williams. Our customer service department will be glad to help you right away. Please hold for just a few seconds and I'll contact our representative for you." *[Receptionist calls Customer Service while caller holds.]*

"Hello, Tom. I have a customer with some wrong-color binders. Will you pull up the records for Mr. Jesse Williams and I'll connect him for you." *[Receptionist gets both Mr. Williams and Tom on the line simultaneously.]*

"Mr. Williams, thank you for being patient. I have Tom Sidell on the line for you. Tom is our binder specialist. Tom, Mr. Williams has some wrong-color binders and I know you'll be able to get his order straightened out for him."

That does take the receptionist a few extra seconds. But it also saves time. Mr. Williams doesn't have to start from scratch, which would only cause his temperature to rise. Tom has a chance to focus on the call, prepare himself, and gather the right records and forms. And, very importantly, neither is dealing with a cold, impersonal stranger. The operator serves as a link and introduces the two, breaking the ice and preparing the way for a positive resolution. This customer will come back. And Tom won't have to deal with a frustrated, upset caller.

Conclude calls with a verification of key points covered. If agreements have been made, restate them now to be sure there are no misunderstandings later.

And finally, use the caller's name. My ongoing national survey of telephone professionals also asks about the techniques others use that survey respondents most appreciate. The simple practice of "using my name" is mentioned more frequently than any other technique.

Apple Computer is one fine example of an organization that's phone conscious. Most companies relegate switchboard operators to lowly respectless positions. But when an operator from Apple attended my Telephone Techniques seminar in New York City, she proudly presented her business card (no different from president John Sculley's) which said, simply: "Aurelia Rae Bove, Customer Relations." Do you provide business cards for your operator? Remember, that one person has more contact with your customers than anyone else in the whole company.

What happens when you treat an operator with respect? I asked Rae about her job. She said, "When someone calls and I answer, I am Apple Computer to that person. Lots of things are beyond my control. But when that phone rings, I have a chance to make all the difference."

At Lotus Development, publisher of the Lotus 1-2-3 computer program, console attendants (switchboard operators) are invited to all important corporate meetings. Are your receptionists and operators treated as the people responsible for vital information centers, or are they always left out?

ARE YOU LISTENING TO YOUR CUSTOMERS?

How many times are we all going to keep on repeating the same thing? Your organization survives and thrives only by keeping track of the needs of its customers. We all keep hearing this, but, as Tom Peters and Robert Waterman note in *In Search of Excellence,* ". . . despite all the lip service given to the market orientation these days . . . the customer is either ignored or considered a bloody nuisance."

Not only does the phone afford an excellent opportunity to poll your customers for feedback, it's also extremely influential in shaping your customers' feelings about you.

QUIT SURVIVING AND SOAR

We can limp along for a while without paying much attention to what our customers are thinking. But to really take off, we've *got* to know what they're thinking, what their (unmet) needs are, and how they size us up. In other words, we need to stay in touch. One way to do that is to hire an expensive market research firm. Or create a direct-mailing program designed to twist your customer's arms until they write you a letter.

Or you can take the easy way. Somewhere in your organization is a group of people who talk with your customers all day long. Maybe it's the telemarketing department or Customer Service. Teach these people to regard every contact with a customer as an opportunity to get feedback.

Of course, people do well only what they are trained to do and are rewarded for doing. Institute a SOAR program for maximum feedback.

S: *Solicit* your customers' suggestions and ideas, actively.
O: *Open* the communication flow with encouragement.
A: *Appreciate* what you hear, good or bad. And say so.
R: *Reward* the behavior of the customers who respond and the reps who listen.

The first step is to conscientiously use each customer contact, time permitting, as a chance to *solicit* input by asking a question or two.

"Thank you for this order. Incidentally, we're always looking for ways to improve our service. Do you have a suggestion or two that would help us do a better job for you?"

"Mr. Adams, I'm putting this order through now. I'd be interested to know if there are related products you'd like us to carry. Is there an item you have a hard time getting your hands on that we should include in future catalogs?"

"I'm very sorry to hear about this error. We do want to improve in every way possible. I'd be very pleased to hear any suggestions you can offer."

"You've been one of my best customers this year and I appreciate it. There's probably nobody better qualified than you when it comes to suggesting ways we can improve our product. If there's one change that would make this product more useful for you, what would it be?"

Although many customers will have nothing to say, it's amazing what great ideas come out when we ask for them. They won't all be earthshakers. But there will be ideas that will make you more responsive to your customers' wishes. The foundation on which excellence is built is input from the marketplace. Usually, you've got to ask for it.

General Electric customers said there was no convenient place to store wines in the company's refrigerators. GE added wine racks to its top-of-the-line models. Many buyers of Jiffy Pop complained that the popcorn was too salty. The company added a salt-free version. Callers on Pillsbury's 800 line kept asking for copies of a bundt cake recipe that had appeared in one ad. There was so much interest in the recipe that Pillsbury formulated a bundt cake mix and successfully added it to the product line.

Once the question is asked, pursue it. Open the communication channel. Often, customers have little to say unless we encourage the flow.

"Please, tell me more . . ."

"I'm glad you're bringing this to my attention. What else happened?"

"That's a great idea! I'll definitely bring it up in our next staff meeting. Is there anything else you can think of?"

The risk of asking for feedback is that some of it may be bad. There's a natural tendency to squelch unpleasant information, but the truth is we've got to hear the bad as well as the good. A good salesman knows that a customer with a complaint will turn into the best long-term customer possible if the complaint is listened to, resolved, and not repeated.

In 1979 the U.S. Office of Consumer Affairs commissioned a long-term study to determine what impact complaints had on customer loyalty. A group of test customers received a phone call asking if there was anything about which they wished to complain. The "control" group received no such call. Some of those who got the call had valid complaints that could not be resolved. Others were resolved.

The interesting outcome of the study is that the least loyal group by far—those who were not repeat buyers over the long term—were those who had no chance to complain, the control group. The most loyal, of course, were those whose complaints were satisfactorily resolved. But even those whose complaints weren't resolved (but were listened to) were substantially more loyal than the control group.

It all makes sense. We hate to be neglected or treated with indifference. Even if you can't truly help an unhappy customer, merely asking and listening strengthens the bond.

Whatever the customer says, *appreciate* it. Even if it's bad news.

> "I certainly hate to hear that we've let a good customer like you down. But mostly, I appreciate that you took the time to let me know about this. Your satisfaction is very important to me. Now that I know about the problem, I can get to work on it. Thank you."

Finally, *reward* the behavior that you value if you want it repeated. This applies to both the customer and the employee who solicits the input. Let your customers know that you appreciate their comments in a tangible way. Certainly, the individual who offers a helpful idea deserves a prompt, personal response, even if it's a word-processed form letter with a real signature. When my wife and I were disappointed with the catering service at Marriott's flagship hotel in Washington, D.C., she took the time to notify the hotel's management of the department's shortcomings. Ten days later, she received a personal letter signed by William Marriott himself. The gracious, appreciative reply ensured that we would return and give the hotel another chance.

The reward may be something quite simple. The computer on which I wrote the manuscript for this book has a horrible keyboard with problems that are well known in the PC industry. Customers aired their views loudly and repeatedly, but the Goliath computer company chose not to listen.

Along came David. A small, market-oriented company in Cornville, Arizona, devised little plastic "keycaps" that glue onto the keyboard keys and make them much easier to use. The plastic they use can't cost over twenty-two cents, but anyone with the offensive keyboard is glad to pay twenty-two dollars to fix the problem. Along with the small plastic pieces comes this slip of paper:

> Thanks to a customer's suggestion, your TOUCH-DOWN Keytops now adhere with a new adhesive for a firmer fit and easier installation. . . . Your comments and suggestions for product improvements are always appreciated. HOOLEON COMPANY.

This company deserves to SOAR. They didn't just listen; they gave credit and reinforced the behavior. I hope they make a bundle.

We need to reward this behavior on our end of the line, too. Telemarketers, for example, are typically paid commissions on the new orders they take. Any time that cuts into "selling" reduces rewards. What happens? Telemarketers transfer complaints to Customer Service. "That's not my job!" Isn't it? Keeping in touch with the customer is everyone's job. But the reward structure doesn't always recognize that reality.

I recommend that every company that wants to *SOAR* institute a reward structure for getting input from the customer. Don't just pay salespeople commissions for their orders. Add a bonus for every helpful suggestion they gather during conversations. When a complaint call comes in, be sure that all phone personnel have handy forms on which to record the details of the situation, spell out the follow-up action, and suggest internal changes that may prevent the problem from happening again. If a sale is worth a ten dollar commission, isn't a completed complaint form that suggests how a problem can be solved and ensures long-term customer loyalty worth much more?

SOARING IN ACTION

Automobile dealers usually aren't thought of as strongly customer-oriented. They tend to be seen as hit-and-run specialists. You buy a used car, or get yours repaired, and they shove you off the lot, so they can start gnawing on the next "mark."

But I've come across one that's dramatically different. South Florida's largest automobile dealer has pioneered an innovative "Customer Care" program that's exactly in tune with the Department of Consumer Affairs study. This organization correctly realizes that satisfied customers are the best possible advertisement for an automobile dealership. They are constantly striving to uncover and eliminate possible problem areas. At the same time, some problems do slip through the cracks. They're determined to hear about them immediately. Here's how this bold new program works:

Everybody who has an auto repaired at this service center gets a personal phone call within forty-eight hours. A staff of three Customer Care specialists and a supervisor do nothing but call customers. With this many dealerships, that amounts to over three hundred calls a day. They simply ask several questions: "Were the repairs completed to your satisfaction? Were you treated courteously? Was your car ready on time?" and so on.

The customers are shocked! They can't believe that an auto dealership actually cares about its customers. But this company does have customer satisfaction as its guiding goal. The people who do talk with Customer Care fall into three categories:

First, there are the customers who were happy all along. In the case of this committed organization, the figure is amazingly high. They're delighted to say they're happy and they're also very appreciative of the attention. You know those people will be long-term customers and will recommend their dealer whenever they have the chance. On future visits for repairs, they often ask to meet the Customer Care person who phoned, just because they want to say "thank you."

Then, there are the few who are unhappy and are anxious to say so. Their common reaction to the call: "You have really got guts to call me!" Other businesses run and hide when customers express dissatisfaction. This one follows through tenaciously until the matter is resolved and the acrimonious customer does an about-face. The key to this program is follow-through. When an unhappy customer talks to Customer Care, he does get a follow-up call from the appropriate department manager.

And finally, there are the customers who are mildly dissatisfied, but aren't about to say so. These people are the "I don't get mad . . . but I'll get even" types. They won't complain directly but they'll tell every colleague and acquaintance they encounter for the next seven years! This is the group that gives Customer Care reps real exercise in tact and diplomacy. Sometimes a customer actually says, "You wouldn't want to hear about it." Usually, it's a quiet reluctance that the reps intuitively interpret as a signal of dissatisfaction. This is where the "O" of SOAR comes into action.

"I really do want to help you with this."

"The whole reason I'm here, and the reason I've called you today, is that I do very much want to know what went wrong."

"Of course I want to hear. Please tell me all about it."

The common reaction is, "You know, I can hardly believe that you really called to find out if I had a problem, and that you are going to take care of it for me!" These are people who will also be customers for life.

The calling program is a huge success and sets a whole new standard for meeting customers' needs. You might think it amazing that there are actually employees who are willing to call hundreds of car-repair customers every week, asking to hear their complaints. That sounds like the most aggravating job imaginable. Surprise! These reps love their work! Actually, they say the position is "very rewarding." They make people happy.

But the most remarkable part of this Customer Care program is not that the calls are made, but that the company does something about what their customers say. A repair department manager can immediately spot lagging performance on the part of any one of his mechanics and augment training in that specific area to eliminate the problem. Get this: *Every single day,* each department manager is given his department's satisfaction ratings, along with its rank among other departments. Every time one department is in the number-one spot five days in a row, the company's vice president personally acknowledges the achievement and gives an award. That's an organization that is SOARing.

THE REWARDS OF SOARing

I'm a frequent customer of an outfit called Long Distance Roses. It's an example of a company that didn't exist a couple of years ago. Today it SOARs because of its great phone manner, consistently reliable performance, fair value, and a demonstrated desire to stay in touch with its customers. I call because they'll deliver a dozen roses anywhere in the United States the next morning, with a gift card, for a reasonable price, they treat me nicely, and I always remember their phone number: 1-800-LD-ROSES.

During a recent call, I was treated well, as usual. The person who answered my call, Susan, was friendly. I knew she was another real person, not just an order-taking automaton. She let herself show, and she was good. She meticulously verified my credit card number, gift card spelling, the works. She chuckled and showed some humor, too.

As is my habit, I told Susan that I was a careful observer of telephone professionals and that she was great. Not many people are truly superior on the phone, and they deserve to know it when they're doing well. Susan was sharp. She said she'd be glad to get her supervisor for me!

Doug, the supervisor, was appreciative and professional. He thanked me for taking the time to report my experiences. And, he asked me if I would please put it in writing. "As a matter of fact, yes, I would be glad to put it in writing, now that you ask."

He had extended a simple invitation, and I accepted. So few people ask you to put your praise in writing. Yet a "good letter" is worth at least hundreds of dollars. It can raise morale and motivate your entire staff toward peak performance. It's the kind of thing that gets held up and read at a sales meeting and saved in a portfolio. Or framed.

Then Supervisor Doug said, "One last thing. We're glad to have you as a customer and I'll tell you what. The next dozen roses you send is on me." I already thought those people were great, anyway. But my loyalty was now sealed.

I was so struck with this company's efforts to SOAR that I did some checking. Sure enough. The company is a total reflection of "stay close to your customers" in action. They sent their first shipment of roses only after extensively researching the market to discover exactly what kind of service people want. They listened when consumers said they didn't know who to call for rapid flower delivery around the country. They lined up a very memorable phone number (800-LD-ROSES). Customers had complained that the old number was hard to track down when they got a sudden notion to send a bouquet. The people staffing the phones in this company are consistently superb. They ask for feedback, and they are rewarded for getting it.

In their first year, Long Distance Roses shipped 15,000 dozen roses. The next year, shipments increased 67 percent. Only 60 percent growth is projected for the third year.

That's the reward when you SOAR on the phone.

6

WIRED EMOTIONS: DEAL POSITIVELY WITH IRATE, DISTURBED, AND DEMENTED CALLERS

Complainer: "Yeah, hello. Say, I bought your training tapes and I want my money back. They're no darned good."

Customer Service Rep: "Hold on a minute. *[Ninety seconds pass.]* "Ah, what is it you want?"

Complainer: "I want my money back. Those tapes of yours are junk. They're kindergarten level with nothin' new in them at all."

Customer Service Rep: "Well, I don't know how you can say that. At least a dozen people a day call just to tell me how good our tapes are."

Complainer: "Look, I don't give a darn about what anyone else thinks. They must be pretty stupid. I've been in this business twelve years and I know what's good."

Customer Service Rep: "Well, I disagree. You don't sound all that sharp to me."

Complainer: "Don't you start insulting me, lady. Now, I'm gonna get my money back if it means—"

Customer Service Rep: "My other line's ringing. You'll have to wait. Listen, you'll have to hang on while I transfer you to—"

Complainer: "No you don't! I will not be shuffled around by some insolent clerk. Now you can connect me with the president of your company, or you can get me my refund right now, little lady!"

Customer Service Rep: "I can't do anything for you. And I don't like being shouted at. Now, if you want to pursue this, you'll just have to send in a letter and explain what was wrong. Our company policy clearly states that—"

Complainer: "I don't want to hear about your company policy and I don't want to hear you. It's not worth my time to write your outfit a letter, but you can be damn sure I'm gonna talk to the Trainers Association about you people. You'll never sell a tape to anyone in Texas, and you're gonna regret what you've just done."

COMPLAINT CALLS: NUISANCES OR OPPORTUNITIES?

High emotions create the biggest problems and the greatest opportunities in business. Problems usually stem from frustrated, disappointed, angry customers who feel let down. They haven't gotten the treatment they feel they deserve and they want you to know it. Most often, the problem is compounded at this point because the company representative reacts personally and emotionally. Instead of being resolved, the problem gets much worse. But emotional calls are potent opportunities if they're handled right.

WHO'D WANT TO HEAR A COMPLAINT?

Anyone who wants to be profitable by preserving long-term customer relationships and by minimizing flak in the marketplace. One Washington, D.C., consulting firm, Technical Assistance Research Programs, has exhaustively studied complaint behavior for the White House, the National Science Foundation, and many prominent U.S. companies. The TARP findings are conclusive and compelling. Complaints are very substantial profit opportunities. The remarkable fact is that any dissatisfied customer who complains about a major problem, one involving more than $100, is at least twice as likely to become a long-term, loyal customer, even when the complaint is not resolved! When it *is* resolved, the figure jumps to six times. And when a complaint is resolved *quickly,* that complainer is more than nine times as likely to become a long-term, repeat customer.

Even when the dispute involves relatively minor amounts from $1 to $5, the complainer is more likely to buy again. When resolution is prompt, he's almost three times as likely to be loyal as the noncomplaining unhappy customer.

Marketing executives generally acknowledge that word-of-mouth promotion can be an important factor in the sales of services or products. But few realize just how important this informal advertising is. Research by Whirlpool and General Electric has indicated that these personal endorsements can carry twice the impact of traditional media advertising. People whose complaints were satisfactorily resolved tell an average of five other consumers about their positive experiences. But those who don't complain tell at least twice that number about their dissatisfaction. This information weighs heavily with their friends and associates when purchase decisions are being made.

"OUR CUSTOMERS MUST BE HAPPY. THEY NEVER COMPLAIN."

Wrong! They never complain *to you.* Every organization has some unhappy customers, but very few unhappy customers take direct action and contact the organization. Consumers cite three reasons in a TARP study conducted for the White House:

1. It's not worth the time and effort.
2. They don't know where or how to complain.
3. They figure that the company won't take any action even if they do complain—that they don't care.

So, instead, unhappy customers simply switch brands, discontinue doing business with the offending company, and start griping to their associates. TARP and A. C. Nielsen research indicates that as many as 98 percent of customers who are unhappy do not notify the company or supplier that disappointed them.

And what about the complaints you *do* hear? Research indicates that for each unhappy customer you hear from, there are at least six other serious complaints you don't hear about, and another twenty to fifty not-so-serious complaints that also escape your attention.

TALK OR SUFFER THE CONSEQUENCES

If the unhappy customer doesn't have a chance to voice complaints, she will first switch brands and not repurchase in the future, and then will tell ten or twelve other potential customers about her dissatisfaction. In fact, 13 percent of those who are disgruntled tell more than twenty others!

To avoid these consequences, give customers an easy way to air their unhappiness. That used to mean providing an address for written complaints. But today a toll-free number is a marketing imperative for companies who wish to exercise good, profitable relations with their customers. Quite simply, Americans have substantially reduced their letter writing. Clairol noted that over a five-year span, from 1976 to 1981, the percentage of complaints that came in by mail plummeted from 60 percent to 9.5 percent. Today consumers expect and even demand a toll-free outlet for their frustrations.

The logic is very clear:

- Some of your customers are unhappy.
- If they don't have an easy way to let you know of their dissatisfaction, they'll quit dealing with you and start telling lots of others that you're awful.
- If they do reach you and complain, they're at least twice as likely to become loyal, long-term customers. And they'll talk about their positive experiences with an average of five other people.

- The more quickly you resolve the problem, the more likely customers are to demonstrate loyalty with long-term repeat purchases.
- They're more likely to reach you if you provide a fast, easy, inexpensive means such as a toll-free customer service or complaint number.
- And on top of all that, it's actually cheaper to handle their complaints by phone. Procter and Gamble finds it 40 percent less expensive to handle complaints by phone than by mail.

There is a very direct, quantifiable benefit to establishing a complaint-handling center and training its staff. By your being easily accessible, the inevitable unhappy customer is more likely to reach you. You benefit by generating long-term revenues, and you also profit by cutting the costs of complaint resolution.

There are also lots of indirect benefits, especially in the areas of product improvements and new product suggestions. Polaroid, for example, listened to numerous complaints from buyers of its early instant-print camera models. Caller after caller indicated that the darn things just quit working after a while. All they got were blank pictures. One of the first questions that Polaroid's Consumer Affairs agents were trained to ask was, "Have you checked the battery?" "Battery? What battery?" Polaroid quickly realized that a major cause of customer dissatisfaction was that batteries had worn out—as is unavoidable—and the customers didn't realize they were supposed to replace them. Very few buyers even realized that the cameras needed batteries.

The Polaroid people might easily have passed judgment on the callers and thought, "These dummies don't even read the instructions." But instead, they listened. And then they reported what they'd heard to Product Development. These recurring complaints directly resulted in the design of the current Polaroid SX-70 film packs, which use built-in batteries that are replaced automatically with each film change.

AN EXAMPLE OF ACCESSIBILITY

The General Electric Corporation is an industry pacesetter in
the field of putting customers first. The GE Answer Center is a
twenty-four-hour facility designed for one purpose: to foster
the "neighborhood store" image for what might otherwise be
perceived as a giant, cold, impersonal bureaucracy. This is an
organization intent on being accessible.

At any one moment, up to 135 telephone professionals handle calls at the Louisville headquarters. GE is so committed to
this innovative concept that it gladly funds this very costly
program—because it's a great investment. The center's phone
bill alone runs to several hundred thousand dollars each
month.

The Answer Center has three major call types, each of
roughly equal frequency. About a third are "prepurchase"
calls from people who have questions to ask before buying
their television, light bulb, or even jet engine. Another third of
the calls are "use and care" inquiries. ("How do I hook up this
darn VCR, anyway?") And another third concern "service"
questions, often from do-it-yourselfers intent on diagnosing
why their twenty-year-old washing machines no longer clean so
well.

Unavoidably, some of the hundreds of thousands of calls do
fall into the complaint category. GE is totally committed to
empathetic handling of complaints. And it pays. GE's extensive quantitative research unequivocally proves that patiently
listening to complaints, empathetically reflecting callers' emotions, and ultimately solving the problems pays compelling,
long-run dividends.

Numbers aside, the most dramatic evidence is the mound of
letters from people whose complaints were well handled.
Those letters usually say something like:

> Ever since my alarm clock broke, I've been mad at you
> people. But when I called your Answer Center, someone
> actually listened and helped me out. Now that I know
> you stand behind what you sell, I'll buy all my major
> appliances from you. And I'll tell my friends, too.

According to N. Powell Taylor, GE's Manager of Customer Service Operations, "Converted complainers are actually much more loyal than any other type of customer. They voice much stronger, positive sentiments and become active, aggressive promoters. They don't just say they like us, they prove it with their purchasing power, and they really do sell their friends and neighbors on GE as a company that sells quality products and stands behind them."

HANDLING IRATE, DISTURBED—AND EVEN DEMENTED— CALLERS

There are three factors necessary in handling complaints well: attitude, skill, and knowledge. Of the three, attitude is by far the most important. And it's not just the attitude of the individual who takes the call: It's the corporate attitude. To be successful handling complaint calls, it's absolutely imperative that top management recognize the importance—and profitability—of handling complaints well. Indeed, the customer service staff, usually regarded as an expensive and resented necessity, is a profit center. Handled well, complainers do buy again and again, and they also become spreaders-of-the-word.

PROMOTING LONG-TERM LOYALTY (AND HEALTHY MARRIAGES)

One of the most impressive complaint-handling innovators is Clairol. Its Department of Customer Satisfaction is doing everything right. Abundant evidence that the corporation truly cares about its relationships with customers is evident starting with the name of the department. I asked Cathi Hunt, Director of Customer Satisfaction how Clairol goes about handling complaints.

"We don't get any complaints," she replied. "About twelve percent of our calls do fit the profile of what most companies consider complaints. But to us, they are either questions or performance issues. Calling them complaints immediately casts a judgment on the consumer voicing either confusion or concern. Even if a customer is unhappy with one of our products because she 'messed up' and didn't follow the package directions, we're talking about a performance issue. We find that people who call with what others may consider complaints are actually our best friends. What they are really saying is 'I want to keep using your product. Please help me with information.'"

The company also demonstrates its attitude by staffing the telephone center with highly trained, motivated individuals. These are not customer service agents, they are Clairol Hair Color Consultants. Each new specialist receives four weeks of classroom training before getting near a phone. That's followed up with one to three weeks observing an experienced consultant in action. Finally, the new specialist graduates to the phone and is closely supervised.

Clairol isn't concerned with just handling complaints; they're out to eliminate the causes of consumer dissatisfaction. The company tracks a large number of statistical variables about each person's performance. For example, if the average "talk time" for one rep is noticeably shorter than for others, the supervisor finds out why. While other organizations may be urging their people to shorten their calls and cut phone bills, Clairol wants to be very certain that the consultant has heard the caller's full story and given appropriate and complete information. When the call concerns the application of a hair-color product, it's very important that the consultant find out what treatment the caller's hair has received recently. If, for example, advice were given without first determining that the caller recently had a permanent, the results could yield a dissatisfied customer. And that leads to lots of negative word-of-mouth propaganda.

Lots of organizations *talk* about listening to their consumers and incorporating feedback from the marketplace into product and planning cycles. Clairol *does* it. The Department of Consumer Satisfaction plays the major role in preparing new product instruction sheets and designing packages. Why? Because they are in the best position to know what consumers really want. When women call and complain about confusing instruction sheets, Clairol rewrites them.

The consultants staffing Clairol's phone lines have prevented many irritated lips (hair-coloring products shouldn't be used on men's mustaches because of different skin sensitivities in the mouth area), saved lots of poodles from looking very strange (human hair-coloring products don't always perform as expected on canines), helped win some county fair ribbons (yes, horse aficionados have been known to spruce up their animals before entering them in competitions), and even saved a marriage! One exasperated husband called and implored, "Please tell my wife it's okay to shampoo her hair. If she doesn't clean it soon, I'm going to divorce her. She read on the package that she should not shampoo after changing her hair color, but that was four weeks ago!"

PLEASE COMPLAIN!

In many instances, companies are best off when they actively promote complaints. One major vinyl-flooring company found that a good many of its customers had problems with their kitchen flooring. Investigation revealed that the most common cause was improper cleaning, which made the floor deteriorate. Buyers didn't read or retain their cleaning instruction sheets provided in each box of tiles. So the company prominently printed its 800 number right on the surface of the flooring. Once the floor was installed, buyers had to call to find out how to clean the phone number off. When they did, they also got complete care instructions that assured long tile life and prevented future dissatisfaction.

If your organization doesn't encourage complaints, it's passing up an opportunity. This is a profit practice most organizations overlook or are simply unaware of. Be certain that from the president to the switchboard operator, everyone is aware of the value of complaints.

There is a groundswell of organizations establishing comprehensive complaint handling and customer satisfaction centers. Although these undertakings are costly, they do yield bottom-line profits. In the case of the progressive Clairol center, the corporate analysts have determined that the center breaks even if only 24 percent of those who call purchase Clairol products in the future. While Clairol won't reveal the results of its research on the actual percentage of callers who do become long-term customers, it's safe to assume that the figure is far higher than the break-even point. Although the investment is, and continues to be, a large one, the Department of Consumer Satisfaction is a dramatic profit generator.

There is every reason for your organization to establish a full-scale telephone center, but that isn't necessary in order to begin accruing the benefits that come from listening to customers. Foster an attitude in the company that customers are to be valued—and listened to. Encourage anyone who has contact with customers to be sensitive to customer complaints; if that employee cannot handle the complaint, be sure he knows how to connect the customer to someone who can. And make sure someone in the company is responsible for keeping tabs on complaints, even if this complaint clearinghouse system is very informal.

Once a complaint-encouraging attitude is developed, we need some tools. With or without a comprehensive telephone center, training is an area where most organizations fall short. Few call handlers get any training in complaint handling. It should not be one-shot deal. Training, reinforcement, and skill development must be ongoing. Certainly, the most accessible phone personnel—customer service reps, switchboard operators, and executive secretaries—all need to develop and reinforce complaint-handling skills with frequent role-playing sessions and ongoing training. Supervisors and managers also must be prepared to handle complaints. The complainers they hear from are even more in need of attention because they've usually "gone higher" after remaining unsatisfied with the response from lower levels of the organization. By this time emotions may be even more wired and wound up.

It's ideal to train "front-liners" so that every unhappy caller is skillfully helped by the first person who answers. When that's not possible, at least ensure that everyone is trained to start heading in the right direction.

> "Mr. Simons, I want to be sure this problem gets immediate attention. I'll make sure our service specialist calls you within the half-hour. I want her to hear the full story directly from you so we can solve this quickly. What number can she call to reach you in the next thirty minutes?"

AN AGENDA THAT WORKS

Depending on how you handle it, the emotional call can be either an extremely positive or very negative experience. Most often, it's the latter. An abusive customer reaches you and rants. You do your best to transfer to somebody else. The call gets worse and you can't get a word in edgewise. In the end, the caller is convinced that you and your organization are as awful as suspected. And you head for the coffee room grousing about what a lousy job this is and how miserable you are dealing with psycho customers.

But on the other hand, handled smoothly, the trouble call results in a stronger relationship with your customer. And more important, you are left with a sense of confidence, competence, and power. When you can handle the emotionally charged caller, you can handle anyone.

Take a methodical approach from the moment you sense that the caller is charged. Keep this agenda by your phone:

STEP ONE: BEFORE YOU DO ANYTHING ELSE, PREPARE YOURSELF

You know if the call will be a rough one within the first few seconds. The caller's tone of voice, accusatory language, and high volume all say, "I'm going to let you have it." How you react at this point determines the outcome of the call. Either you shut off and get defensive, or you decide to handle the call positively.

Complaint Call Agenda

1. Prepare Yourself
   - Check your body posture.
   - Grab some paper and a pen.
   - Commit to the "Adult" behavior state.
2. Listen Rationally
   - Hear all they have to say without interrupting.
   - Provide oral feedback to let the other person know that you're "there."
   - Record notes as they talk.
3. Establish Rapport
   - Use the other person's name.
   - State your purpose, which is to solve the problem.
   - Indicate that you have jotted notes.
   - Ask questions to gain further clarification.
4. Create the Solution
   - Ask what the caller would like.
   - Speak in positives.
   - Sell the solution.
5. Confirm and Close
   - Review the agreements you have reached.
   - Use terms that express mutuality.
   - Be explicit about next steps.
6. Follow Through

Check Your Body Posture   We've already covered body posture in chapter 4, "Power Talking." It plays a critical role when handling emotional calls. Forget the misconception that you and your voice are separate entities. You reflect your whole being in the way you speak. The best impression you can convey to a caller is that you are interested, concerned, open, and ready to help. Be sure your body shows that attitude and it will carry through to your voice. It will also impact the way you think.

The "closed" posture quickly communicates indifference and disregard. Avoid folding your arms, crossing your legs, and yawning unless you wish to indicate disinterest. The "open" posture shows your willingness to accept information. Uncrossed limbs, erect posture, and an overall alertness mean that you are ready to listen. This same posture translates through your voice. To sound alert, look alert. Although the other party has no direct eye contact, they do detect your attitudes through the sound of your voice, and that's influenced by your body's posture.

Although alert body posture can be "heard" by the other person, its influence on you is even more important. The physical act of adjusting your body gives your inner self a signal that you intend to manage your behavior instead of just letting it happen.

Grab Some Paper and (Get Ready to) Take Notes   Emotions don't solve problems. Facts do. You're about to get a barrage of facts. Capturing them on paper offers several advantages:

- First, taking notes keeps your focus on the content of the message, not on the person, his voice, or his emotions. The more senses you involve in absorbing new information, the better you understand it. Writing brings into play your visual senses and your motor responses.
- It's always useful to have a written record of your conversation for future reference. You may even avoid future legal action by maintaining accurate notes. (I recall averting a nasty legal showdown with a seminar company president in just this way. His story had changed from one call to the next. I believe that the single most important factor in his decision to drop this matter was my set of precise phone notes. I didn't just say, "Last time we talked, you said . . .", but instead, my records allowed me to say, "When we spoke at nine-twenty, your time, on June third,

you said—and I quote—" His lawyer advised him to forget the matter.)

- Finally, taking notes conveys an important attitudinal message to the caller. When they finish "dumping," you're able to say,

> "I'm glad you've brought these facts to my attention. They are very important, and I've jotted down some notes just to be sure I've heard you correctly."

It's just as if you were saying,

> "I'm not brushing you aside or taking you lightly. I care about what you are saying and I've taken the trouble to be conscientious about hearing you."

Commit to the "Adult" Behavior State   Transactional Analysis was pioneered in the 1950s by the American psychologist Dr. Eric Berne. But its validity isn't limited to psychologists or Americans. TA is a fundamental explanation of how all people interact with each other. Each of us has three basic behaviors available at all times:

"Child" is the first behavior you learned as an infant. It's the part of you that's focused on expressing emotions (usually without regard for their consequences). When the person you speak with is mad, glad, sad, or scared, he or she is exhibiting Child behavior.

"Parent" behavior is what we pick up from parents and parent figures. It's based on the belief that there is a "right" way to do things. And if you aren't doing them that way, you get scolded. You are hearing Parent behavior when a customer gets judgmental and says, "What's wrong with you? Why can't you get this right? If you weren't so stupid . . ."

"Adult" behavior reflects the problem solver in us. When we put emotions and judgments aside and concentrate on analyzing the facts of a situation, we're showing Adult behavior.

The problems with emotional calls stem from the behaviors we use in reacting to them. Parent behavior most commonly gets a Child reaction; Child gets Parent:

Parent: "I don't know why you stupid people can't get this straight. Can't you read? Again, you sent my shipment to the old address. Are you just dumb, or what?"

Child: "Don't blame me! It's not my fault. Somebody over in shipping must have screwed up."

Or, the other way around:

Child: "I've had it with you! No! I don't deserve this kind of treatment. You &&*%%%###$! . . ."

Parent: "Watch your language! You should know better than to talk like that."

The Child-Parent and Parent-Child routines are two of the most common games people play. They're totally unproductive and make things worse, never better. We get so used to being unconsciously sucked into these games that it feels like we have no choice: "That guy made me so mad when he called me stupid that I had to hang up on him. What else could I do?"

But what really happened is this: The customer called you stupid. Maybe mean Uncle Ralph used to call you "stupid" and you have a sensitivity to the word. Hearing it reminded you of Ralph, twanged a nerve, and you took it personally and got angry. That caller didn't *make* you angry. He merely sent some impulses into your phone. You *chose* to react angrily.

When you're in your Child behavior mode, you feel hurt, angry, sad. When you're in the Parent role, you feel self-righteous and judgmental. But, in the Adult role, your personal feelings are shelved; your judgments about others are held in abeyance. All you do is gather information, analyze it, create solutions, and solve problems.

You get into the Adult role as a matter of choice. You make the conscious decision that you are going to remain emotionally neutral and withhold judgment. You stay focused on the objective and factual content of the message, and ignore the caller's emotional messages. It's not easy.

STEP TWO: LISTEN RATIONALLY

This is the key. Problems can be solved only after gathering information. You're about to get a flood of information. Much of it is emotional, some is objective fact. The critical task in defusing irate callers is to listen. And remember, it's an active process. Erect, attentive body posture first. Then, paper and pen, complaint form, computer screen, or some other means of recording the information that's streaming in. Conscientiously recording that information helps keep your attention focused on it.

"But I really *shouldn't have to* listen to that *jerk* after swearing at me that way. I mean, *it's just not right* to talk that way."

Who's talking here? Parent. Parent doesn't want to listen. Parent wants to judge and determine what should and shouldn't happen; what's right.

"Hey, I just don't *feel like* listening to these irate callers. They either *make me angry* or they bore me to death."

Now who's talking? Child's concerned primarily with how he feels.

Only the Adult role gets you listening. Adult isn't concerned with "should" or "feel." Adult cares only about one thing: "What will solve this problem?"

Hear All They Have to Say Without Interrupting   Before they phone you, those irate callers pace around for a while. They fashion hard-hitting speeches. Real tirades intended to pummel you and put you down. They repeat their speeches over and over in their heads, improving on the pungency. When the speech is really ripe, the best thrashing they can muster, they call. They're proud of their speeches. They're going to "let you have it." Not because it will do any good. Not because verbal abuse is effective. Just because they feel hurt, wronged, frustrated, disappointed, let down. And because they've designed and rehearsed such a beautiful speech.

You can forget saying anything like, "Just a minute, now. Stop where you are. You're getting out of hand and I don't want to listen."

It's as if they have bulging lava domes of anger all built up inside them, and they just have to vent some of their hot gases before they explode. The gas has to get out. Let the whole eruption happen. It doesn't hurt you because you aren't in the Child mode. It doesn't allow you to make judgments about the callers, because you aren't in the Parent mode. It just gives you information so you can get to work solving problems.

Provide Oral Feedback to Let the Other Person Know That You're "There"   Rude complainers rarely single you out as the recipient of the only complaint they'll ever lodge. Sometimes they're chronic complainers. They complain frequently and have discovered that the response they're most likely to get is bored disinterest. So they keep on complaining, louder each time, hoping to be heard. And finally, they reach you.

After many episodes of being ignored, they're bent on getting through to someone. You're elected! They are so accustomed to rejection, rude responses, and getting the runaround that they have their emotional volume turned way up. They just want to get through.

You can completely change the outcome of these calls by *listening,* and it's very important that you let the complainer know that you're listening; that you're not giving the typical runaround response. Low-level oral feedback is the best way to do this. Don't interrupt, but do provide soothing, encouraging sounds and statements that let the caller know that you are taking in all that she says. "I see . . . and then what happened? . . . uh-huh . . . go on . . . I'm with you . . . please tell me more . . ." Your use of low-level oral feedback lets the caller know that you sincerely are listening, and that means calmer emotions and more information.

There are two goals you're out to achieve at this time. First, you want to work through the emotional parts of the agenda. You want that volcano to blow itself out so that you can move ahead. Second, you want to gather information that will allow you to solve this problem, and prevent it from happening in the future.

You accomplish both goals by listening. Listening silently just makes the complainer think that she's being ignored once again. As long as you remember that the information you're getting—though negative in tone—is valuable, you can stay positioned in a receptive stance, ready to hear more. It truly is valuable. The venting of emotions will defuse the caller and let you pass through the unproductive emotional backwash and get on to the solutions, and it will provide you with a good start in your information-gathering process.

Record Notes as They Talk   Hearing a complaint is the truest test of listening skills. Your rejection mechanisms are in high gear and the defenses are up. There is a very high risk of not listening at all. So use every tool available to listen as effectively as you can. None is more effective than recording notes.

Because complaint handling is such a high-risk, high-payoff situation, it warrants an investment in tools. Design a form that allows you to stay on track with the response agenda. It's a convenient way to be sure that you aren't straying from careful listening and that you're covering the right bases in the right order. Using a complaint form reminds you of the bottom-line purpose of every complaint-handling episode: Solve the problem and prevent it from recurring.

STEP THREE: ESTABLISH RAPPORT

Complaint calls start off with emotional expressions. Solutions reside in the rational realm. How to get from one to the other?

First, be sure that the emotions have run their course. Then build a bridge to rational discussion. That bridge-building process is your conscious effort to establish rapport. The most important rapport-building technique is simply consciously wanting it. The steps come naturally so long as you remain aware that you are guiding the complainer through an agenda that leads from emotional expressions to rational solutions.

Use the Other Person's Name   Dale Carnegie was right. There is no sweeter sound to any person in any language than the sound of his or her own name. Use the caller's name and you immediately lay the cornerstone for a bridge of rapport. The most effective problem solvers use a personal approach. Begin bridge building by addressing the complainer by name (in moderation) after hearing all she has to say.

State Your Purpose: To Solve the Problem   Most of the time, a person who fields a complaint call is actually wishing the caller would go away. The last thing that person truly wants is to hear and solve the problem. The complainer knows this and naturally assumes that you are like everyone else.

You make headway only when there is true commonality of interests. The caller may think that your interests are quite different. He figures that you want to give him the brush-off. But you don't. You're different. You want to solve this problem. So, say so!

> "Mr. Thompson, thank you for taking the time to let me know about this situation. My highest priority right now is solving this problem with you. I will personally work with you until it's all straightened out. Your satisfaction is important to me and to my company."

In effect, you are saying,

> "You and I are on the same team. You may be used to company reps who try to wriggle away from your problems and who treat you as a nuisance. I'm on the other side of the fence: your side. Let's pool our energies and work together."

Indicate That You Have Taken Notes   Your aim is to show the caller that you have a sincere interest in solving the problem and that you have been listening. Reinforce your assertions with evidence:

> "I'm concerned about this situation, and your experience is important to me. I jotted some notes as you were talking because I want to be sure I understand exactly what happened."

Suddenly, the caller is getting the idea that you actually mean what you've said. If you took the trouble to record notes, maybe you actually do intend to understand his side of the story and take some action.

Ask Questions to Gain Further Clarification   Odds are that the caller gave you a blow-by-blow that was laced with emotion and delivered in stream-of-consciousness fashion. It probably was not a carefully structured account. And no doubt there are a few holes to fill. Asking questions about them helps you gather the information you need to create a solution. And it does something even more important: it reinforces the skeptical caller's dawning belief that you may really mean what you said.

> "I want to be sure my notes are completely accurate so I really understand what happened to you and how I can best help. You mentioned that the shipment arrived on the seventeenth. Did you first notice the damage right away, or was it after you opened the carton?"

STEP FOUR: CREATE THE SOLUTION

Here's where we lose track of our roles. We get the feeling that we're "on the line," all alone, thrown into the position of quickly coming up with a solution that must soothe the complaining customer.

But wait. Are we alone? We've been telling and showing the caller that we are on his side. The caller wants the problem solved. Isn't that exactly what we want? Don't we want to preserve our relationship with this customer? And don't we also want to get to the root of the problem and prevent it from happening again?

We want the same thing as the complainer: a solution that produces satisfaction. We've got a problem-solving partner. Consult that partner.

Ask What the Caller Would Like

"Mr. Thompson, I know you've already given this situation a lot of thought. Please tell me what would make things better for you. I'm not exactly sure how to handle this best, but I am sure that you've got some good ideas. What would you like to see done?"

Quite often, we're cringing at the prospect of refunding the customer's money, compensating for time and trouble, or providing some other costly solution. And when we ask the complainer what he or she wants, it turns out to be much less formidable a solution than we were prepared to create. Lots of times, the complainer simply says, "I want an apology," or "I just wanted you folks to know about this. I feel much better already."

Since your ultimate aim is to win back the dissatisfied customer, it makes sense to ask the customer what he or she wants. Surprise! It may be much less than you were prepared to offer.

Speak in Positives   In the "Power Talking" chapter, we explored the tremendous impact that language has on perception. When emotions are running high, as in complaint situations, word choice is critical. There's an emotional world of difference between:

"I can't do anything but send out a serviceman and I can't do that before next Wednesday,"

and,

"I'll be glad to dispatch our service specialist. I will make sure that repair is scheduled for Wednesday, if that's a convenient time for you."

Sell the Solution Regaining the faith and continued business of a disgruntled customer is a selling process. The "product" is the solution or action we've promised. But the inherent value, or benefit, of that solution may not be clear to the complainer. Make it very plain.

"Mr. Thompson, having that unit repaired on Wednesday means that you'll still be able to complete your production run by the end of the week. And by repairing the unit in place, you won't have to readjust the connecting belts. Of course, your original guarantee will still be in effect. Our service specialist will also be able to inspect the mounting on the unit and check for any vibration that could cause other problems in the future."

STEP FIVE: CONFIRM AND CLOSE

The wrap-up phase in the complaint-handling agenda is the confirmation. Because emotions have been running high, it's quite likely that your understanding and the complainer's don't quite mesh. This is a high-risk, high-reward situation, so it's well worth confirming your mutual understanding.

Review the Agreements You Have Reached The last thing you ever want to hear is, "You promised to do so-and-so, and you didn't come through. Now I've *really* had it!" Carefully review the steps you have promised to take, as well as any action the complainer will be taking.

Again, language is important. Reinforce the "same-team" orientation by using terms that indicate mutuality. Rather than saying,

"I want to be sure that you understand what I'm going to do . . ."

say,

"Let's be sure we both are clear about what we'll do next . . ."

Of course, the more explicit the better. Confirm exactly what you'll do, what you are expecting of the complainer, when it will happen, and so on.

"I'm going to contact the dispatcher right after we hang up. I will confirm that the repair specialist will be at your plant on Wednesday morning by nine-thirty. Meanwhile, you'll shut down the power to this unit on Tuesday evening. On Wednesday morning, our man will meet your maintenance supervisor at the South Gate, and you'll leave clearance so he can get through security. I will call you before five on Tuesday to let you know the service specialist's name. Are we in agreement on everything?"

STEP SIX: FOLLOW THROUGH

Now, *do it.* There are lots of times when you may fall slightly short and be forgiven. Solving a complainer's problem isn't one of them. It is absolutely imperative that you take precisely the action you've promised, and that all other parties are apprised of the situation. As soon as you hang up, record in your calendar each step and exactly when you're going to take it. To coordinate with others, again speak in positives: not "When can you get to this?" but, "I'll need confirmation on a Wednesday morning job. I'll be glad to hold while you arrange it."

In most instances, you should issue a written confirmation of the solution you have agreed to. Always thank the customer for taking the time to help you improve your service or product. The written follow-up gives you another opportunity to create a positive impression that will help mend the damaged relationship.

Complaint Handling Guide

	Date	Time
Caller's Name:	____	____

(Phonetic Spelling):

Company: City:

Phone Number: (   )   Extension:

Time Zone:

Your Name:

1. Prepare   ____
   Alert posture; turn away from distractions. Stay
   in "adult" frame of mind.

2. Listen   ____
   Offer feedback, encouragement. Take notes.

3. Create Rapport   ____
   Empathize; offer apology. Use caller's name.
   State your aim: Serve as partner to solve this problem.
   Ask questions: "When did things start to go wrong?"
              "How could we do a better job for you?"

4. Create Solution   ____
   Ask what the caller wants done. Explore options.
   Think about the value of this relationship in the
   long run.

5. Confirm   ____
   Be sure you and the caller have the same
   understanding. Verify all addresses, numbers,
   spelling. Review joint agreements.

	Completion	
	Date	Time
6. Follow Through		
What immediate action did you promise?	____	____
Whose cooperation do you need?	____	____

Complaint Handling Guide

When was personal thank-you note sent?   ____ ____
Is this relationship worth a follow-up phone call?   ____ ____

What would have prevented this problem from happening?

What can we change or improve to be sure this situation doesn't come up again?

PLACATING LANGUAGE

As always, word choice is critical. Even though your intentions may be positive, you doom yourself to failure during conflict resolution when you use phrases like:

"I *disagree* with you. You'll just *have to* fill out the paperwork first. You really ought to *compromise* on this. Now, according to our *company policy* . . ."

One after another, negative, option-eliminating phrases like these limit our chances to explore and find viable solutions:

"Disagree"   A prime offender. Our culture is thoroughly imbued with a black-white, right-wrong outlook. We don't often leave much room for multiple options, each with its own merits. "Disagree" may leave your lips meaning only: "I don't see things exactly as you do," but by the time it reaches the listener, it has become, "You are wrong!" Or worse, "You're lying!" Though not intended, this is the meaning that the listener invariably "hears." Not the ideal starting point for problem solving! It's much better to say,

"I understand your point of view, and there may be another way to look at this I'd like to consider with you."

"Have to" Predictably, people back away from anything that's forced upon them, even if it's good. "Have to" is an option-limiting, coercive phrase that is best avoided. You can almost sense the listener stiffen when you dictate what he'll *have to* do.

Use open-option phrases that encourage participation in creating the solution. "One thing we may consider doing here is to . . ."

> "I understand what you're telling me and I do see your viewpoint, Mr. Thompson. It certainly has merit, and I have another point of view, too. By carefully noting all of the special circumstances in a brief report, we'll be able to examine this particular situation. I'll be glad to help you through the paperwork, and then we can explore the options and come up with a solution that meets your needs, as well as ours."

This really says the same thing as the option-limiting "You'll have to do the paperwork" approach, but creates alternatives, doesn't antagonize, and sets the stage for an open-minded solution.

"Compromise" Like "disagree," this word evokes a not-necessarily-accurate meaning: "Give in." The complainer feels quite justified in her position. Most likely, she is absolutely convinced that she's right. As soon as you say "compromise," the listener thinks you're really suggesting at least a partial cave-in. Her thought may be "But I know I'm right. Why should I compromise and give up ground?"

Instead, use phrases that don't imply defeat or concession. "Let's explore our options and look for ways to satisfy both of our needs."

"Company Policy" Poison words! This phrase immediately conjures the image of an unimaginative, unthinking, green-shaded clerk thumbing through a thick manual full of inflexible rules. When he finds the paragraph that applies to our situation, we're dead. "The book says we have to do this. Don't bother me with facts or circumstances."

Every situation is different and does warrant individual consideration. Even if you must follow the policy guidelines, state it in a way that shows that you have weighed and considered the circumstances. "Mr. Thompson, in this particular situation, I recommend that we agree to . . ."

Compare this scenario with the same situation at the beginning of chapter 6.

Complainer: "Yeah, hello. Say, I bought your training tapes and I want my money back. They're no darned good."

Customer Service Rep: "Sir, I'm sorry to hear you were disappointed. I'll be glad to help you. What is your name, please?"

Complainer: "Sam Colby. And I'm the director of training at Silo Systems, plus a board member of the Texas Training Association, so I know what I'm talkin' about."

Customer Service Rep: "Mr. Colby, my name is Sarah Linnet. I'm glad to hear from you. You're obviously an expert and I'd be grateful to get your feedback."

Complainer: "Well, I don't mind tellin' you that those training tapes of yours put me in an embarrassing situation. I played them at our monthly meeting before I had a chance to listen first. They were so basic everyone just laughed."

Customer Service Rep: "That does sound awful. Please tell me more about what happened."

Complainer: "Well, our people are pretty well trained right from the start. Your tapes were way too basic. You should have heard the comments."

Customer Service Rep: "Please tell me—"

Complainer: "Well, pretty near everybody, even the newest employees, said that the material was too darn simple. In fact, it's just about what we teach rank recruits in their first two days here."

Customer Service Rep: "I see."

Complainer: "I mean, what we need is an advanced training program, not just another refresher on the kindergarten stuff."

Customer Service Rep: "I understand. What else would you like to tell me about the tapes?"

Complainer: "Nothin' really. I just don't think they're worth a penny as an advanced training aid. And I want my money back right now."

Customer Service Rep: "Mr. Colby, I'm sorry that you were disappointed with the tapes. I can imagine how embarrassed you must have felt when your employees started laughing. My number-one concern is satisfying you, and I'm sure that I can help you with this situation."

Complainer: "I'm glad to hear that. Most folks these days try to give me the runaround."

Customer Service Rep: "Not me, sir. I'm glad you called and I value your expert opinions. I jotted some notes as you were telling me about that meeting and I'd like to be sure I got them right. Did you say that your first training days cover material just about the same as the tapes cover?"

Complainer: "That's right."

Customer Service Rep: "And you also mentioned that every one of your employees goes through that training program. How many people is that?"

Complainer: "About six or eight new ones each month."

Customer Service Rep: "I see. And many of your employees really need advanced training on an ongoing basis, is that right?"

Complainer: "Yes, ma'am. And if I could just find an advanced program, I'd buy a dozen sets a year."

Customer Service Rep: "Mr. Colby, the program you purchased actually is our introductory course. I'm not surprised that your trained employees found it pretty basic. We do also offer three advanced modules that pick up where your introductory program left off."

Complainer: "Gee, nobody told me about them. Maybe you could send me one for a preview? But I'm not gonna pay for it!"

Customer Service Rep: "I'll be glad to. And as for the introductory program, how would you like me to handle that refund?"

Complainer: "Well, you know, you gave me an idea a while back. With the number of new recruits coming through here, I could actually use that program in place of the first training day. It could kinda get the new folks started before the classroom stuff begins. I might just hang on to 'em. But I'll never play them for experienced employees again, you can bet on that."

Customer Service Rep: "That sounds like a plan that could actually lower your training costs."

Complainer: "It might at that."

Customer Service Rep: "Mr. Colby, I just want to be sure we're clear about what'll happen next. I'm going to send you a preview set of the three advanced modules today. There will be no charge for the standard thirty-day preview period. I'll call you in two weeks to find out what you think of them. You're going to hang on to the introductory program, so we won't be issuing a refund. Have I got that right?"

Complainer: "Yes, that's the way I see it, too. You know, you've given me an idea or two here and I appreciate it. If you'll send a supply of catalogs for your other training tapes, I'll give 'em out to the Texas Training Association members. You sound like a pretty good outfit. I guess I shoulda listened to those tapes before I played them at the meeting. They'll probably be just right for the newcomers."

Customer Service Rep: "I'll be glad to send as many catalogs as you need. I've enjoyed talking with you, Mr. Colby. You've given me some good ideas, too. I look forward to hearing your reactions to the advanced program."

This example isn't farfetched. The opening line was the same as the exchange at the beginning of this chapter. The outcome was dramatically different solely because of the way the complaint call was handled. Following the complaint call agenda can be one of the most profitable things any organization does.

7

PHONEGOTIATING: REACH WIN/WIN AGREEMENTS BY PHONE

The word "negotiate" conjures up images of cigar-chomping union leaders in a showdown with management, a manicured financier finalizing a leveraged buyout, or a State Department official attempting to secure the release of hostages. We usually think of negotiating as overcoming an obstacle or bringing two disparate positions together.

Negotiating is the process of reaching agreement with others. It's something we all do every day. When you work out agreements with vendors, you're negotiating. Salespeople negotiate constantly. Whenever you want someone to do something for you, you're negotiating.

WHAT CAN BE ACCOMPLISHED BY PHONE?

Although negotiations are usually thought of as face-to-face affairs, almost any matter can be negotiated by phone.

When George Burns has an idea for a new book, he doesn't hustle off to sit with an agent or a publisher. He tells his personal manager about the idea. His manager calls his agent. His agent calls the publisher and describes the idea behind the book. Sometimes it takes just a few minutes. The publisher loves the idea and says yes to the agent. They agree on an advance fee and a courier delivers contracts for all to sign. The entire negotiation takes place with a few phone calls.

When Harold Weisbrod, chairman of the largest jewelry manufacturing company on America's West Coast, wants to acquire another jewelry company, he mounts a relationship-developing campaign using a series of phone calls spaced out over months. When he decides to open a factory in Bangkok, labor negotiations are carried out by phone from his penthouse in California.

When an advertising agency wants to stretch its client's advertising budget, it phones the television networks to negotiate "opportunistic buys." Sometimes minutes before a program is to air, commercials may be scheduled for discounts at up to 50 percent from the normal rate. It's not unusual for a minute of network advertising to cost $500,000, so these last-minute telephone negotiations result in huge savings.

When the FCC mandates that Capital Cities/ABC must spin off more than a billion dollars in broadcast properties, a phonegotiator like Howard Stark starts dialing. The super media broker says, "I'm just as comfortable doing business around the pool at the Beverly Hills Hotel or at the Racquet Club in Palm Springs or the Coral Beach Club in Bermuda or in Palm Beach. All I need is a telephone."

STRENGTHS AND WEAKNESSES OF PHONEGOTIATING

Negotiating by telephone is definitely different from negotiating during face-to-face contact, but it's not necessarily less effective. In fact, there are some real advantages to telephone negotiating.

WHAT YOU LOSE

True enough, you do lose many nonverbal aspects of negotiating. Most successful negotiators interpret body language, gestures, and facial expressions and give them at least as much consideration as the words exchanged. In face-to-face meetings, nonverbal behavior may even be more important than words. Although you may say, "That doesn't seem like much of a problem," I may observe your neck muscles tighten and your fist close, both signaling that you feel very bothered indeed.

On the phone you can pick up pronounced signals like "smiling" voices or tense, combative postures. But it's impossible to accurately read the more subtle nonverbal signals. When the other party is silent, it may mean that he's carefully considering your point and is about to indicate agreement. But it may also mean that he's about to hang up.

Without nonverbal cues, negotiators are much more likely to misunderstand each other. Because negotiating is essentially a communication process, it's incumbent upon both parties to take extra steps to assure clear understanding. Telephone negotiators also lose part of the interpersonal dynamics that result from eye contact, handshakes, and so forth. Indeed, some see the telephone as an inherently impersonal communication medium.

Unless the stage is carefully set, there's also a real risk of being distracted or losing your train of thought. Because your counterpart can't see you, it's easy to get sloppy, glance at other work, make eye contact with people passing your office, tap your fingers, or slouch down in your chair.

WHAT YOU GAIN

The telephone does offer some strong advantages, though. One of the biggest problems in negotiating occurs when people get sidetracked and focus on personality showdowns rather than the facts. When negotiating by phone, taking careful notes, it's easier to remain focused on the objective business at hand. Face-to-face negotiators feel awkward if they're constantly writing while the other person is talking. On the phone, it's easy to do so without appearing rude or self-serving.

Another advantage of phonegotiating is that it avoids the

common pitfall of sessions that should be private involving just two principals becoming group encounters. The vice-president's assistant, an outside consultant, your VP of product development, all detract from concentrating on the issues. As one very high-ranking ad agency executive points out, "Some people just don't function well in meetings. They have a compulsion to grandstand and pontificate, whereas they're quite reasonable and down to earth on the telephone."

In large meetings, much of the negotiators' energies are channeled off to winning the group's sentiments over to one side or the other. On the phone, it's easier to stay personal, concentrating on just the other person, or possibly a few others via teleconferencing. Even when several people are involved in a joint telephone hookup, each individual essentially functions on his own. There's far less showmanship and much more productive discussion.

Phone negotiations tend to be shorter than in-person meetings. When we travel to a negotiation, we seem to stretch the session out, almost as if we're justifying the trouble we've gone to. It is less likely that there will be rambling small talk on the phone. We get down to business more quickly.

When any negotiation bogs down, or an impasse is reached, it's often best to take a breather and resume later with fresh thoughts. It's much easier to cut off a discussion by phone than when you're sitting around a boardroom table or sharing a meal.

And it's also easier to say no when you aren't looking your counterpart in the eye.

FUNDAMENTAL SKILLS

Negotiating effectively by phone is simply a matter of practicing the fundamental strategies that work so well with in-person encounters and being extra sure that you communicate clearly to compensate for the increased risk of misunderstanding. These include listening, speaking to be understood, approaching the negotiation with the proper attitude, and, of course, the key to any negotiation: trusting your instincts.

LISTENING

Compensating for phone shortcomings begins with listening more carefully. Be sure distractions are eliminated and that you're writing notes during the session. But even with all of your attention focused on the discussion, you may misinterpret what you hear because so much of the nonverbal information is missing. Use the feedback loop consciously and frequently when negotiating.

"Mr. Bennets, I want to be sure I'm understanding you correctly. Are you saying that the building's policy prohibits weekend move-ins and that I'm therefore in violation of my lease?"

Don't limit the feedback to matters of fact. Verify your impressions of the emotions involved, too.

"I feel as if you may be a little annoyed with me for tying up the elevators. Have other residents been complaining, or are you simply feeling afraid that I won't be taking my lease agreements seriously?"

Remember, the simple fact is that we're all pretty poor listeners. Many negotiation breakdowns are the result of misunderstanding. Be sure you're dealing with the right information before reacting to it. The best insurance is a deliberate feedback loop to verify what you think you heard. Review the "Listening" section of Chapter 3 (page 69) for more details.

SPEAK TO BE UNDERSTOOD

The fundamental aim when speaking during a negotiation should not be to win or prevail, but to be understood. Successful, lasting agreements result from common understandings of both viewpoints, yours and your counterpart's. Rather than coercing the other guy to concede, aim to have him truly understand how you see things so that the agreement you jointly arrive at will reflect your mutual interests.

"Mr. Bennets, you may agree with my decision or you may not. I do want to explain why I scheduled a weekend move-in so you will understand that I wasn't acting in bad faith."

Understanding isn't the same as agreeing. Agreement comes after you both understand each other. Acknowledging that you understand the other party's point doesn't mean that you're giving in to it or agreeing with it. Both parties should adopt an attitude of being equally involved in the process of deciding an outcome and satisfying mutual interests. Careful listening and clear understanding will result.

ATTITUDE

The mental framework that gets positive, winning results is not confrontation. It's cooperation for mutual gain. Approach the negotiation as a shared task. Both of you want the same thing: to come out ahead.

One way to think of negotiating is as an exercise in creating abundance where there appears to be scarcity. Approach with the attitude that the pie can be made bigger, not that you're going to outsmart the other guy and get more pieces than he gets. You do this by first gathering information about his needs and comparing them to yours, seeking areas of mutual interest, and building on them. View your counterpart as a partner in a creative process.

INSTINCTS

Besides having good listening and communication skills, and along with keeping a creative, winning outlook, it doesn't hurt to have good instincts.

My literary agency is a father/son team. Arthur, the father, brought his young son into the office one Monday to "see what the business is like." A call came in concerning a publisher's advance on a sight-unseen book. In this very unusual situation, the first-time author and the publisher already had a strong relationship. The publisher had offered $100,000 for the right to read the manuscript first, before any other publisher saw it.

The manuscript had been given to the publisher for a forty-eight-hour review over the weekend. Now, the publisher was calling to say, "We all love it. How much money will it take to pull this book off the market and give us publication rights?" Artie signaled to his son to pick up the other line, silently listen in, and get a taste for the phonegotiating process. Of course, the publisher balked at the figure and said he couldn't possibly go that high. The green, untrained son signaled to his dad to put the call on hold. Then he said, "Dad, don't move one cent. I can tell by his voice that he's going to accept the deal unchanged."

Now Arthur was in a spot. Of course, he wanted to reach a fair agreement, and he also wanted to respect his son's input. So he gambled and stuck to the figure, saying, "I have the other nine copies of the manuscript here in the office. What I'll do is send them around and we'll just have to see what happens."

The publisher wanted the book very much and quickly recanted, agreeing to pay the full advance Arthur had requested. A lot of negotiating isn't book-learnin'. Instincts play a huge role in developing rapport and knowing just how close to the brink you may get before falling in.

BEFORE YOU CALL

Telephone negotiating skills come into play long before you dial. The most successful negotiators credit their successes to meticulous advance preparation. The work begins well before the call. In fact, the time taken to prepare for a negotiation should exceed the session itself. Here's where novice negotiators fall down. They may simply pick up the phone with a half-congealed idea of what they want to accomplish and expect to think up strategy as they go along.

If an issue is important enough to negotiate at all, it's important enough to negotiate correctly. Think of the time you put in before the call as an investment, not an expense. The gains that result from careful preparation are measurable and often dramatic. Since a large part of the negotiating process is bringing two people to understand each other's viewpoints, that's where the preparation begins. Well before the session, carefully list:

Your viewpoint, and the other party's. You've got to know "where he's coming from" to understand his motivations. Negotiation is an empathetic process. Get into his shoes and imagine yourself looking at the situation as he does.

Your goals, and the other party's. Of course, you start off with a pretty good idea of what you want to get from the negotiation. But what will the other party be seeking? Most current negotiation literature revolves around the concept of win/win. Agreements that persist over time are those which benefit both sides. During the negotiation itself, you're going to ask the other party what he's after. Start now by anticipating what his aim is likely to be.

The fears and concerns you both face. Fears are best dealt with out in the open. Both sides are afraid that they may not get a "good deal" or that they'll "lose." Address this downside by analyzing what the other side is probably afraid of. That way, you'll be better able to empathize and directly reassure your counterpart that it doesn't have to be that way—for either of you.

The concessions you may be willing to make, and what your counterpart may concede. Both parties generally start off selfishly knowing what they want and aggressively going after all of it. Ultimately, enduring agreements result from a give-and-take process that may—in the end—leave each party better off than they had originally hoped possible. Weigh the concessions you may have to make. Consider what the consequences will be. But also be prepared to suggest concessions the other side may make. In particular, search for those that benefit you but "cost" the other guy little or nothing.

The other person's interests and needs as well as your own. In most negotiations, both parties have firm positions in mind. But those positions are only ways of satisfying underlying interests and needs. There are undoubtedly other ways of satisfying those fundamental needs and they may not even resemble the positions you started shooting for. During the negotiation process, one underlying aim is to turn up new approaches to satisfying each party's needs.

Rob Rutherford, a national negotiating authority who leads workshops around the country, has prepared a "Successful Negotiator's Perfect Planner" that should be thoroughly prepared before any session. It's five solid pages of questions. It includes these points and others. And it's a good example of the rigorous preparations that are the hallmark of fruitful negotiators.

This kind of extensive preparation is helpful under any circumstances. But by phone, it's even more critical. Time frames are compressed when negotiating long-distance, so each minute has a higher value. It's more difficult to recover from a stumble. Since there's less time, it's particularly important to assemble alternatives and give them creative consideration before getting the call underway.

SETTING THE SCENE

Before placing a negotiation call, it is critical that you set the stage by eliminating any possible distractions. Lock your door! Be certain that your secretary clearly understands that nobody is to enter, no calls are to come through.

In the course of daily phone conversations, you may be only slightly distracted when someone enters your office and slips a note in front of you. When negotiating, you can completely lose your concentration. It may break your thought processes, or chip away at the rapport you've developed. And that may have dire consequences.

Your field of vision should include only the written goals you're working toward, your preparatory analysis of your interests and theirs, and a note pad. And don't forget your mirror! The expression and posture you see in it is being communicated by your voice. Anything else isn't germane and draws away your attention.

DURING THE CALL

Another fundamental doctrine of effective negotiating is to separate the people from the issues. This critical principle is covered in depth in *Getting to Yes*. Roger Fisher and William Ury wrote this fantastic negotiating guide as a result of their work with the Harvard Negotiation Project. I highly recommend it. The people and the emotions they feel must, in fact, be dealt with before getting down to the facts.

EMOTIONS COME FIRST

"If I hadn't dealt with the emotions first, we would never have closed the deal." Real estate brokers know that nothing is as emotional as the sale or purchase of somebody's home. Carole Kelby, top salesperson for Coldwell Banker's Chicago office for many years, recalls a specific instance where she had to be an emotional miracle worker.

She had an offer to present on a lovely home whose owner had gone out of town without advising his broker. He was tracked down (with much effort) while vacationing in another state. His broker, the listing agent, called the owner with Carole in the office. He began, "We have an offer for you and you don't even deserve it. You should never leave town without telling me how to reach you . . ." and continued, "You're not gonna like this offer, but here it is anyway. Here's Carole, the agent who represents the people who are making this offer."

What a horrible introduction! When Carole picked up the phone, she knew that she had to address emotions *first*. Her opening words were, "Mr. Jones, thank you for the opportunity to present this offer. It was a pleasure to show your home and I can feel all the TLC you've obviously put into it over the years."

The seller thanked her for the compliment, but was still stiff from the listing agent's reprimands. "First, let me tell you about *your* buyer." She very consciously used "your" to start forging a link between the two principals. The listing agent had already set Carole up as "the enemy who wants to steal your home with an unworthy offer," so Carole didn't say "my buyer" and avoided the risk of sullying the buyer by association. She proceeded to explain how well qualified the buyer was, and how closely the buyer's desired timetable matched the seller's. A thirty-day escrow had been requested; ideal for the seller, who had already purchased another home many miles distant.

So far, she had nearly overcome the damage done by the listing broker in the opening minutes of the call. She put a finger to her lips indicating that the not-so-savvy listing agent should remain silent. "Mr. Jones, the price your buyers are offering is $390,000," said Carole.

The other agent cut in, "See, I knew you wouldn't like it!"

"You're damn right I don't. I won't take a cent less than $400,000," said the owner.

This home had been listed for six months without a single offer. The seller was moving to the new home and would soon be saddled with two mortgages. The offer was just 2½ percent below the listed price. This should have been a guaranteed deal! But the lister's clumsy handling of the emotions behind the numbers threatened to squelch the sale.

Carole had to work a miracle. "Mr. Jones, I will do my best to get the full asking price for you. First, please allow me to play devil's advocate and throw out some thoughts. This buyer is very well qualified and will get a mortgage without any complications. His preferred escrow period is short, which works to your advantage.

"If I'm not successful and this buyer goes ahead on the other home he is considering, you may find a new buyer right away. But it's most likely that he'll want a sixty- or ninety-day escrow. That means you'll have two mortgages to pay while you wait for escrow to close, assuming all goes smoothly.

"And were you aware that, because of vandalism risks, your insurance rate will jump substantially if the house is vacant for more than thirty days? And of course, with winter coming, you'll have snow-removal costs. Mr. Jones, I will do whatever you decide. If you'd like me to ask your buyer to consider increasing his offer, I will."

This time, Carole didn't just put a finger to her lips, she

glared at the other broker so that he wouldn't again blow the deal.

The seller did accept the offer, realizing that it would cost him more to delay than to accept. He also thanked Carole for her professionalism.

What turned this apparently jinxed negotiation around was Carole's deft handling of the important emotional issue. First, she repaired the damage her colleague had done and sought to establish rapport by complimenting and thanking the seller. Then, she formed a subtle link between the two principals. Without telling the seller he was using bad judgment, she offered additional information that let him conclude, on his own, that he should rethink his position. She planted a seed of doubt and fear with the legitimate mention of vandalism insurance costs. But she also let the seller "save face" by adding, "I'm glad I mentioned it, because most people don't realize what these insurance companies do when a house is unoccupied."

Had Carole focused on the facts alone, or let herself be dragged down by the other broker's bumbled handling of emotions, there would have been no transaction.

FOCUS ON THE LONG RUN

One of the keys to successful negotiating, whether by phone or face-to-face, is to focus on the long-term relationship. We rarely seek to reach agreements that only affect a single person or event. More likely, you'll have repeat business encounters with a person after you successfully reach a positive understanding. Keep your sights focused on the long-run big picture.

One of my seminar attenders recounted an incident with a long-term customer. The company sold metal washers in large quantities, and this customer had been buying for years. One 200-pound shipment of #10 brass washers had been carefully checked, logged, and shipped as usual. The customer telephoned to report that the shipment she'd received was a 100-pound carton. She reached the shipping department of the firm. The clerk who answered was polite but officious, "I'm sorry, ma'am, but I've checked our records and I'm quite sure that 200 pounds were shipped." The customer was sure that it had been only 100. Ultimately, the company charged for the full 200 pounds and insisted that the invoice be paid. They got the extra $320 the clerk insisted the customer pay, but they lost a customer who'd been steady for three years.

On the other side of the coin, one of my consulting colleagues ordered a $2000 computer printer from a mail-order firm in Texas. When it arrived, he carefully unpacked the box and found that it was missing the interface cable that connects the printer to the computer. The packing slip did show that the cable had been included, so he phoned the supplier. The mail order representative said, "I just can't see how the package would have gone without the cable. It shows on our copy of the packing slip and it even has a checkmark beside it." My colleague agreed, "That's exactly what my packing slip shows, but there is no cable in the box."

The mail-order supplier wisely replied, "Well, I don't see how this could have happened, but your satisfaction is what's most important to me. I will have the cable expedited this afternoon."

Not only does my colleague buy all of his computer supplies from this same outfit, he also purchased a second printer from them and recommends the firm to his colleagues. Had they charged him for that cable, the result would have been dramatically different.

My literary agent stepped in to act as an arbitrator when a high six-figure negotiation had reached an impasse. A well-known author's first book had been on the *New York Times* bestseller list for twenty-one weeks and the publisher had done a terrific job promoting the book and the author. Now, the author had completed a second book. Again, it had the markings of a smash hit. The author wanted to work with the same publisher. The publisher wanted the author's second book. They both wanted the same thing.

But the author wanted a bigger advance than the publisher was willing to offer. The negotiation was dead in the water, stuck in rigid positions: "We won't pay more." "I won't accept less."

Enter the arbitrator. Wisely, he focused not on differences or positions, but on common interests.

"The author understands your point of view and he doesn't want to hurt your long-term relationship. It worked well on the first project, and we all believe that we'll come out ahead on this one, too. We're not out to squeeze you. We've got a very good idea of what this author's work is worth to other publishers, but we don't even want to try getting it because our relationship is more important than the money. We want to continue the relationship and we believe that it's in both of our best interests to work together on the basis of this fair figure."

The negotiation was successful mainly because of the agent's repeated emphasis on long-term interests rather than short-term dollars.

ESTABLISHING TRUST AND RAPPORT

Before dealing with objective facts, it's important to be sure that you've developed comfort and rapport. Focusing on emotions is one good way, and there are others. Refer back to "Wired Emotions," especially page (125). You'll want to be sure that you're using your counterpart's name, that you monitor your body posture, and that you ask plenty of questions to ensure that your counterpart realizes that you want to understand his viewpoint.

The essential foundation for a mutually successful negotiation is trust. Once trust is shaken, the entire negotiation process is imperiled. Negotiators with foresight agree on the absolute need for truth and honesty. If caught in the slightest misstatement, the entire negotiating process is undermined. Even if there is no chance that you'll negotiate again with this specific individual, everyone knows everyone else these days. We're all connected. Treat me poorly, lie to me, or abandon ethics and it will haunt you. This isn't just karma talk. Our world, and especially our country, has shrunk dramatically, largely because of telecommunications. Word gets around.

INTERESTS AND NEEDS VERSUS POSITIONS

When emotions have been dealt with, rapport built, and the scene set for long-term relationship priorities, you're prepared to move ahead with the objective aspects of the negotiation.

Approach the negotiation as a shared task. You both are looking for the same thing: an agreement that meets as many of both parties' needs as possible. The starting point is the needs themselves. About the best way to move into this phase is to explain your needs and offer your thoughts on what the other person's needs are that you've already thought of. There are more. And you only find them out by asking.

Suggesting needs you've already considered and asking about others you haven't are strong ways of showing the other party that your concerns and aims are not purely selfish. Of course you want to meet your needs, but you're interested in the other party's, too. This extends the rapport upon which the whole negotiation is founded, and it also keeps the negotiation headed in the right direction.

You aren't arguing to forward or defend your own position, you are both creatively seeking solutions that meet both sets of needs.

NONCONFRONTATIONAL LANGUAGE

As we all know, what you say isn't as important as how you say it. One of the most important language guidelines to keep in mind is the absolute need to avoid confrontation. Review the phrases in "Wired Emotions" (see page 132) and ensure that terms like "compromise," "have to," "disagree," and similarly charged expressions are eliminated from your vocabulary.

Another valuable language guideline is to "speak from the I." Saying "you" leads to interpretations and defensive reactions. Stick with facts. "I feel let down" is a fact and correctly recognizes the source of emotion. "You let me down" is heard as an accusation and begets a refutation. "I really feel disappointed that we had confusion on this matter" is a fact nobody can argue. "You led me to believe those terms were okay" is a matter of interpretation and is likely to get a defensive reaction, especially on the telephone, where you cannot communicate through body language, facial gestures, or the tactile signals that could soften the impact of your words.

TIMING AND REINFORCEMENT

The outcome of most negotiations is largely determined in the first few minutes. If there's to be a counterproductive standoff between combatants, that's usually apparent in the first exchange or two. If both parties are negotiating for mutual gain, that shows right at the start, too.

We all respond to positive reinforcement. When the first move in a negotiating exchange is going in the "right direction," reinforce it immediately.

"Bill, I knew that we'd be able to work this out together. I like the progress we've made already. You're a pleasure to negotiate with."

And if your gut is telling you that things aren't going too well, trust your instincts. It's not likely to get better, so take control.

"Bill, I know we had scheduled this afternoon as the best time to finalize our agreement, but I'm not concentrating as well as you deserve. I've got a few distractions at my end, and this may not be the most convenient time for you, either. Let's both let it rest for a day and take it from the top tomorrow when we're both fresh. Is this same time convenient, or would you prefer to have me call before lunch?"

It's much better to begin anew with healthier attitudes than to attempt getting a derailed negotiation back on track midway through.

CALL RECORDS

One top New York City negotiator I interviewed admitted he had a secret weapon. In high school, he had been a shorthand champion. To this day, he records thorough notes during all negotiations. Whenever one party relies solely on memory, and the other has written documentation, the latter clearly has the advantage.

A Colorado-based real estate syndicator explained how a single page of notes was worth a lot of money to him. He'd been involved in an apartment building partnership in another state and had agreed to buy out the other partner's interest. On checking with the lender, he was assured that the interest rate would remain unaltered, there would be no assumption fee, and the basic terms of the loan would not change. Once the title change was recorded, he received a letter from the savings and loan indicating that the interest rate had increased from 8 percent to 14 percent, that "points" would be charged for the title change, and important changes would be made to the loan's acceleration clause.

The syndicator retrieved his call log and called the lender's senior manager responsible for the transaction.

"Somehow we've had a miscommunication here and I'd like to straighten out what happened. I may have misinterpreted something we discussed by phone, and I just want to understand how such a major difference of understanding could have occurred. I'm looking at my call log here for January twenty-third. I called you just past two P.M., my time. Why don't I hold while you get your log for that date. It would have been just after one o'clock, your time. Let's see what your notes indicate."

Of course, the lender had no log. Documentation always prevails over recollections. In this case, the value of that single call log was $43,000.

AFTER THE CALL

Immediately after any telephone negotiation, send a "Memorandum of Understanding" that restates the agreement you've just reached. Call logs are great; follow-up memos are better still. Sending a letter that puts forth your understanding of the agreement places the burden of refutation on the other party. When you send such a letter, include a phrase along the lines of: "I've done my best to summarize the points we covered and agreements we reached with this memo. If I've misunderstood anything, please do respond so we can be perfectly in tune." If they don't, your version prevails.

Sometimes, these memos have been known to cover points that weren't actually discussed. A national authority on negotiating himself cites a phone call in which he contracted with the best-known national management education association to present a series of seminars. He got busy and just didn't get his follow-up memo prepared that day. In fact, as is often the case when we don't do something immediately, it didn't get prepared the next day. Or the next.

But the association *did* send a memo of understanding, including a section limiting the lecturer's right to sell books during the programs. This hadn't been a part of the original phone conversation. But calling now to say, "Hey, I don't recall talking about that," seemed a bit distasteful, so he put it off. And off. Of course, the association's written memorandum prevailed, and the lecturer forfeited the several thousand dollars he usually earned in book sales after his lectures.

UNUSUAL PLUS

If you're truly concerned with the long-term relationship, take a few minutes to employ this rarely used technique. After your agreement has been reached and both parties are satisfied, let it sit for a day or two, and then call again.

Cement the good feelings that result from a fair, double-win agreement by calling simply to say you enjoy doing business and that you're pleased with the outcome.

And you may consider using the plussing technique. During that call, ask if there's a way the agreement might be made even better, now that you've both had a day to think about it. The other party will be taken by surprise, so you'll need to offer reassurance.

"No, I'm not calling because I want to change anything we already agreed to. It's just that sometimes, after thinking it over for a day, people think of one more thing they should have asked for or included, but overlooked. I really meant what I said about valuing our long-term relationship. And if there's a way to make you even happier about our agreement, we'll both benefit. Have you thought of anything you'd like to add?"

Fine-tuning and polishing your negotiating skills, careful preparation, and, most important, nurturing a positive win/win attitude all constitute the phonegotiation process.

8

DIALING FOR DOLLARS: COLLECT PAST-DUE ACCOUNTS AND CUT BACK ON A/R PROBLEMS

Salesmen usually get most of the credit when companies are profitable. Their efforts are directed toward increasing revenues. But lots of high-revenue companies sell themselves to bankruptcy. The profit game takes many players with complementing roles. Among the *least* celebrated players are the phone specialists who handle collections in Accounts Receivable. And yet, they have a much greater potential impact on profitability than sales forces.

Consider a company with annual sales of $1,000,000, and net profits of $50,000. Suppose that company normally writes off 2 percent of its receivables as uncollectible. If an effective A/R Department cuts the bad debt margin from 2 percent to 1 percent barely an eye blinks. There's certainly no hoopla.

But wait! Cutting bad debt from 2 percent to 1 percent, that is from $20,000 to $10,000, for that million-dollar company with a 5 percent net profit has exactly the same result as increasing sales by 20 percent. And you can bet there's a lot of celebrating when the Sales Department turns in a 20 percent sales increase. But nobody in A/R goes to Rio or gets a Seville if bad debt is cut in half. Let's look at the numbers: A 20 percent increase in sales is $200,000, of which $10,000 is profit. Reducing bad debt from 2 percent to 1 percent of the total $1,000,000 also yields $10,000—which goes right to the bottom line.

The most powerful tool in A/R is the telephone. According to Paul Overton, manager of the collection division of the Credit Managers Association, "Letters simply don't work anymore, no matter how sophisticated you make them." Calling to collect a past-due account is a clear case of goal phoning. And to tap the full power of the telephone, you've got to practice conscious contact.

WHO PAYS THE BILLS?

No company ever decides to pay its debts, or decides anything else for that matter. A *person* decides to send that check. Most often, it's a manager in Accounts Payable, but it may be a president, or controller, or even a secretary who expedites a voucher. The people who make these decisions all did the same thing last Friday. They all went to the bank and deposited their paychecks. Then they went home with their deposit receipts and put them next to a stack of bills. During the weekend they all took the rubber-banded stack of bills, totaled them up, and discovered that the amounts owed were larger than the paychecks they deposited. Then they all sorted out the bills and decided which would get paid and which would not.

First, they pay those they must because the creditors have recourse. The landlord will evict them; the water company will turn off the tap; the bank will repossess the Buick. Then, they pay those that are costing too much to delay. The credit cards with the highest interest rates get paid next.

And finally, there are lots of bills left and very few dollars. The creditors who have established personal contact called, developed rapport, and maybe even "bugged" their debtors a bit to get paid. The aged, anonymous bills whose creditors aren't charging interest and have no recourse don't get paid.

And then, on Monday morning, these people go to work and do exactly the same thing with their companies' bills.

Managers responsible for collecting accounts are always looking for ways to create recourse opportunities and ways to charge interest. What they don't often do is design a system for establishing personal contact with debtors, developing rapport, and "bugging" them. And of course, they don't generally train the Accounts Receivable clerks to use their telephones as profit tools.

PROMPT PERSONAL CONTACT

After legal recourse and interest charges, nothing is as effective as prompt personal contact when it comes to collecting past-due accounts. And that doesn't mean sending out lots of photocopied collection letters with drawings of executioners on the letterhead. (No fooling, one of my Canadian clients sent out letters that read, "Unfortunately, Ray, the prayers didn't work, so I'm using this as a last resort." The Credit Manager, Margaret, really did draw a masked executioner with a double-edged axe in his hand. I liked her artistic touch. She colored in several red drips on the side of the chopping block! I keep that letter in a frame.)

SCORE!

Collecting Accounts Receivable is a game. It has four quarters. The first quarter is called "Notification." Companies send invoices and statements to notify their accounts that they must pay for whatever they bought. Some companies devote a lot of attention to their notification strategies and tactics. They design attention-grabbing invoices; send copies to everybody at the obligated company; add personal notes in the margins; stamp "Your Prompt Payment Is Appreciated" all over them, and do pretty well. Lots of companies don't give much thought to this first notification quarter. They don't score.

The next quarter is called "Reminder." Most companies wait until they're really sure that their invoice was ignored, and then they mail another one. The computer generates a statement each month, and they send that, too. If they haven't yet scored, the outcome of the game is already in doubt.

The third quarter is called "Discussion." Most people don't want to talk to the debtors because they feel uncomfortable. They might not know what to say and they might have to face failing. So they wait a good long time before attempting to score. Their chances are getting slim.

The final quarter is called "Compulsion." It's also called "Unpleasant, legally costly encounters with people who will never buy from you again." It's called "Give a big chunk to the collection agency." A factoring agent may pay only a few cents on the dollar for these accounts. This last quarter is also called, "You haven't scored yet? Forget it!"

There's just one way to win the collection game: Score early and eliminate any procedure in your collection system that drags out the process and depersonalizes contact. To collect a higher portion of the money owed you, sooner, look for ways to speed up the collection process, make it more personal, and shorten the game.

That's why *Phone Power* is important in Accounts Receivable. The telephone lets you have personal contact with your debtors and convey a sense of urgency.

DON'T DIAL YET

Whether you're calling to land a job, negotiate a contract, close a sale, or collect a past-due account, the fundamental principles of power phoning are the same. Start by doing your homework. The Accounts Receivable people who don't experience success are people who belatedly and haphazardly call long-delinquent accounts, say whatever comes to mind, and go on to the next call.

To succeed at "Dialing for Dollars," spend more time planning each call than you spend on the phone. And then maximize that investment of time by following up immediately after the call is complete. The call itself, while critically important, of course, should occupy less of your time and attention than the planning, preparation, and follow-up.

PRECALL PLANNING

Check What's Been Done to Date   Review the dates and notes from previous collection calls. Scan the letters that have been sent. Confer with the salesperson assigned to this customer and see what recent information you can pick up. Knowledge of the past and current facts, together with a plan for handling the call dialogue, will yield a payment commitment.

Be Certain That There's a Problem   First, review the payment records. Is this a chronic situation, or an isolated instance? When was the company invoiced, and what reminders have they had? It's possible that they haven't even been billed. Verify—positively—that your company isn't at fault. If the account has been paid, or if there's a customer service problem, and you call to berate the errant debtor, you will severely damage the business relationship. Be sure the check didn't come in the morning's mail before placing the call.

Be Sure You Know Who to Call   If your records don't indicate previous collection calls, you should call now just to find out who is responsible. Call the account's switchboard and ask who heads Accounts Payable. Then ask for the name, hours, and the secretary's name of the individual authorized to pay past-due invoices.

Plan Your Dialogue   A script—whether written out verbatim or in a simple outline—is invaluable in keeping you steadily on track. You want to steer the call, so have a road map that helps you navigate. The key element of the dialogue guide is excuse handling.

Don't lock into a script that someone else has written.

You've got to personalize the words so that they sound natural from you. Try out various introductions and probing questions until you discover the approach that feels good and works.

Set Your Objectives   Not just one, but a hierarchy of objectives. Your goals are to collect as much as possible, as soon as possible, of course, but you also want to experience some measure of personal success with every call.

Primary objective: Your primary objective is to get a reliable commitment to satisfy the entire past-due amount immediately. Of course, this is what you really desire, and what you attempt to get. But be realistic. Mitigating circumstances may make this impossible. If you're collecting from an individual who has lost her job, or a company that just had its contract with the Department of Defense canceled, you won't get full payment immediately, no matter how good you are. If you have this "pay it all now" objective as your sole target, you're setting yourself up for failure. That means you won't achieve your personal success goal. And you're also not pursuing the course that will achieve your goal of taking in the maximum dollars.

Secondary objective: To collect the highest amount possible, and give yourself the best shot at succeeding, be prepared with secondary objectives, as well. That's plural. The key with secondary objectives is to offer options, each of which is of roughly equal value to you. The person from whom you're collecting may have a strong preference for one of the alternatives. And the important thing is that he will have chosen the repayment plan which best suits him.

Bottom-line fallback: When you achieve neither your primary nor secondary objectives, it's tempting to throw up your hands and decide you'll give it another shot next month. There are two problems with this: First, you aren't achieving the goal of collecting as much as possible. In the long run, a debt that gets no payments fades further away from possible collection each month. The likelihood of collecting anything, ever, diminishes steeply. Second, the goal of experiencing personal success is also unmet.

It's just plain human nature to avoid unfulfilling work. Everyone wants a positive self-image. It's common to give up when you fail to achieve your primary and secondary objectives. After several failed calls, the voice in your head starts saying, "I'm really not too good at this 'Dialing for Dollars' stuff. I haven't made a speck of headway all day. Maybe I'll just send out a bunch of letters."

Set an easily achieved bottom-line objective for every call. It may even be, "If nothing else, I'm going to get this Accounts Payable clerk to send through authorization for a one-dollar payment."

Why bother with very small payments? Three good reasons:

1. Psychologically, you give yourself reinforcement. You set out to achieve one of your objectives, even if it wasn't your most preferred. You get to conclude your calls with a string of successes instead of failures.
2. Psychologically, you've gotten the debtor to acknowledge that he has an obligation and an obligation to meet it. You maintain some control. Six months later you'll be glad to have a series of one-dollar payments instead of a debtor who says, "I don't remember this at all. I don't believe we owe you this money." Or worse, "Well, Simon's no longer here and I have no record at all of owing you anything."
3. Legally, you're way ahead. Should the debtor experience severe difficulties, your debt will take priority over those which have no payment records.

Set a tangible bottom-line fallback for every call and be determined that you won't hang up until you have achieved it.

GOTCHA WITH THAT ONE!

One of the most effective defensive moves in the "Don't let them score" game is "Ha! Threw you with that excuse, eh?" It's been said that one of the biggest lies in the world is "The check is in the mail." To be effective on the phone in A/R situations, you've got to be prepared to handle any excuse. First, you want to find out if it's the truth or a stall. If it's a stall, you'll want to overcome it.

The problem is, we usually don't know how to respond when an excuse is served up. So we say, "Oh, okay then. I'll look for it in this week's mail." About two weeks later we realize we've been had and get up the nerve to call again. After three unreturned calls, you finally get through and hear, "Gosh, our computer has been so fouled up . . . Oh, I said that the time before last? Ahhhh, would you believe our bookkeeper has been out all week?"

There's one simple, highly effective tool for handling excuses on the phone. It'll take a capital investment of about $2.29. Go to the drugstore, head for the stationery aisle and get a pack of 3″ × 5″ index cards. Then, look for the aisle where they sell photo albums. Find the page inserts that have clear plastic sleeves layered vertically on the page so that you can flip each picture up and see the one mounted underneath it. Be sure that the sleeves overlap slightly with the bottom ¼″ or so of each picture showing. If the company budget can take it, invest in a three-ring photo album, too. On the cards write down every excuse you've ever heard. Ask the other A/R clerks for the wildest excuses they've heard, too. Across the bottom of each card, write a condensed version of the excuse: "Computer's broken," "Bank goofed," "Bookkeeper sick," and so on.

Then, brainstorm. For each excuse come up with a simple, direct question or two that will give you a good idea whether the summarized excuse is true, or just a stall. Then write the question on the main upper portion of the card.

Now slip those cards into the sleeves so that you see each of the excuses showing through the ¼″ overlaps. Whenever you hear an excuse, you scan down the cards, flip up the one that pertains to that excuse, and read the question.

Your array of cards will grow as you hear new excuses. The questions you have written out will change and improve as you use them. Eventually, you'll end up with a couple of pages in your photo album propped up in front of the phone. As soon as you hear an excuse, you're set to respond immediately and return the punt.

"The check is in the mail."   "Oh, great. For my records, I'd like to get the check number and the date it was mailed. That way I'll be watching for it and won't have to bother you. I'll be glad to hold."

"Our bookkeeper has been sick all week."   "I'm sorry to hear that. He must be feeling lousy. Which hospital is he in? I'd like to send a get-well card." (Don't laugh. If he is in a hospital, the minute you take to write a card may ensure that your bill will be paid the day he returns. If he's not in the hospital, ask how long he's been out, and who's handling Accounts Payable in his absence.)

"We've run out of checks."   "That happens to us sometimes, too. You just can't tell when the new ones will be delivered, either. I'll have one of our salesmen in your area swing by and drop off a blank counter check in the morning, or would you rather write a check on one of your other accounts?"

"The bank screwed up our account."   "Gosh, that must really be giving you a few headaches. I always find that banks will get off their duffs and fix things up faster if they get a few phone calls. I'll be glad to take a minute and let them know it's important to us, too. What bank do you use and who handles your account there?"

"I'm pretty sure that was approved and sent along for payment."   "Oh, great. Say, I don't want to take any more of your time tracking it down. I'll check with the next person down the line, myself. After it's approved, who do you send it to?"

"We're in the process of moving the office and everything's been boxed up."   "You'll probably need a couple of days to unpack, so I'll call and remind you next week. I can send a messenger by your new office to pick up that check. When is the move scheduled to take place?"

Feel like you shouldn't have to track down paperwork once it's in the other company's channels? Or that you shouldn't have to send a messenger to pick up a delayed check? Or that you shouldn't have to hold while they fetch a check number? You don't have to, unless you want to be sure of scoring.

I know people with fertile imaginations and nimble fingers who have nearly a hundred cards in their albums. They score lots of points early in the game.

READY, SET, DIAL!

Just before you place the call, focus on your objectives, glance in your mirror—yes, your body posture and tone of voice are just as important in A/R calls as in any other—and check your attitude.

Be on guard and stamp out the first sign of an attitude that says, "I hate calling these deadbeats. They always lie to me and they never do what they promise." Instead of pointing that finger at "them" focus your attention on the three curled fingers pointing back at you. Your attention should be centered on yourself; what improvements can you make to your collection techniques so that the averages improve and you score more, earlier?

GUILT AND JUDGMENTS

Blame has no place in collection calls. It's counterproductive. Don't judge the debtor; negotiate with him. Refer back to "Phonegotiating" and look for ways to creatively come up with mutual gains. Look through the other guy's lenses. How will he come out ahead by paying this bill? What are the benefits he'll gain? Be ready to point them out.

Hospitals have a terrible time collecting from uninsured patients. A credit manager from one of San Francisco's major hospitals complained that there was nothing she could offer as a benefit and that the hospital really did not have any leverage. It was prohibited from turning away patients with past-due accounts.

We discussed her situation during an Accounts Receivable seminar and agreed that she could offer a benefit after all. While it's true that the patient would be treated, regardless, she found her collection calls much more effective when she said, "Sticking with this payment plan will mean that you can always rely on us to treat you in any emergency. Isn't it good to know that you'll be able to count on quick attention and the right medication when you need it? That's exactly the kind of peace of mind you get by paying this bill as we've agreed."

Always assume that you're calling simply to arrange a payment plan with someone who does want to play fairly. Don't start off thinking that you'll have to coerce. It'll show in your voice.

LAY THE GROUNDWORK

Chances are that your contact won't be available on your first call. Review conscious contact strategies for winning in "Phone Tag" and "Opening Doors." When you do connect, be sure you're talking with the right person. If you haven't spoken before, but the switchboard gave you this individual's name as the right person, make sure it's correct. First, introduce yourself and identify your organization. Say it slowly and deliberately. You want to establish a personal contact with the other party, so he's got to know who you are. Then, ask the first question:

"I understand that you are the person authorized to pay past-due invoices, is that correct?"

Now state the true purpose of your call. The truth is that you're calling to find out why you haven't received payment.

Don't judge at this point. Don't presume that you're speaking with a deadbeat. Just ask the next question:

"Dave, I'm calling to find out why we haven't received payment on our July ninth invoice."

Be quiet! You want to know why. You've asked the question, now wait silently for the answer. Zip your lips, even if it means eight seconds of silence. Control the call by putting the "other guy" in the reactive mode. Don't presume that you're being dodged. Give the other guy a chance to respond. You may hear what you're looking for. If it's, "the check is in the mail" or another possible excuse, flip up the appropriate card and move ahead.

Listen carefully and hear more than just the words. Is the person simply disorganized, but well-meaning? Does he sound apologetic? Is he defensive? Is he trying to snow you? You're probing for information now. If you hear something that suggests there may be a severe problem, proceed with nonjudgmental, nonaccusatory questions.

"What have been the biggest changes in your business conditions recently?"
"Have there been personnel changes in the department that may have slowed things up?"

Go fishing. Find out where you stand. If you learn that the company is in trouble, you've got all the more reason to press for some payment now. You want to be on top of the stack when the bills are sorted out. Get there by making prompt, personal contact.

SELL YOUR PLAN

Remember, you're not calling to "make him pay his bill." That can't be literally accomplished in a phone call. What you are out to achieve is a commitment to repay according to an agreed plan. And you're going to reinforce the commitment to make sure it's kept. But first, you've got to sell your plan. Only one thing motivates people: self-interest. Show the other party that it's in his best interest to pay the bill. Talk benefits. You're no different from any other salesman, except that you face a tougher sale.

Naturally, you begin by going for your primary objective. If you determine that it will not be possible to achieve full payment now, be prepared to achieve one of your secondary objectives.

PRESENT ALTERNATIVES AND LET HIM CHOOSE

A lawyer friend of mine prepared a "Money Purchase Pension Plan" for an entrepreneurial client to file with the IRS. The small company didn't do well. Since its contributions to the plan would have been mandatory, the president decided not to file the plan after all. Filed or not, the attorney had done his job. The client couldn't pay the $2500 legal fee, because the small company was floundering. It was going to pay office rent and wages before it paid the lawyer.

Rather than being stuck with just the primary objective, "Send the $2500 today," the attorney had prepared fallback positions.

"Richard, I understand that things are rough for you right now. The last thing I'd want to do is force you into something that would shut down your company. That would end our relationship, and I want it to continue for years.

"The total amount you owe is $2500, and I understand that it's not possible to pay that all right now. There are a couple of other ways we can go that will satisfy the obligation, and make sure that you stay in business, too. One way is to make monthly payments of $250 for ten months with no interest charges added. That'll keep your cash flow smooth with small, even payments.

"Or, if it's more convenient, you could send me $625 at the end of this quarter and each of the next three quarters. That leaves you plenty of time to plan ahead.

"You may actually prefer to eliminate a major chunk with a $1000 payment now. Then send another $750 in six months, and the final $750 at the end of the year. That would let you make rapid progress right away with not much obligation remaining.

"Richard, you're the one with the best picture of your cash flow projections. I do want to make this as convenient as possible, so you tell me which plan is best for you."

The idea is to have the debtor "own" the payment plan. You've invited him to participate in planning his destiny. You're far more likely to get compliance if the person feels that he had a hand in creating the plan and that it takes into account his business realities.

MUTUAL CEMENT

Having reached an agreement, even if you had to back off to your bottom-line fallback, cement it. You aren't just after a commitment. You want to do everything possible to ensure performance. That begins while you're still on the phone. Use the feedback loop and speak in terms of mutuality.

"John, I feel good about *our* agreement and the plan *we've* come up with. I jotted some notes during our conversation and I want to verify that I clearly understand how *we're* going to proceed."

Of course, thank the other person and let him feel good about what has happened.

FOLLOW-UP IS MOST IMPORTANT

You may have hung up, but the call isn't over. Immediately update your notes and be sure that your files are current. Be certain that you record the dates for next steps and enter a reminder in your master calendar. If you made an appointment to call again, be positive that you keep the appointment. If he has agreed to send a check by the 15th, make a note to call on the 13th and remind him. As the American Collector's Association says, "There are two pillars of effective collecting: Persistence and Follow-up."

CONFIRM IT IN WRITING

Put synergy to work. Use mail to reinforce the call. Restate exactly what you've agreed on as a workable payment plan. Send the letter in the same day's mail. And include a photocopy with a stamped envelope. Ask the debtor to initial a copy and return it for your files. Every time that person takes any action that acknowledges the debt and signals a good-will intention to repay, you're stepping in the right direction.

FOLLOW-UP REMINDER SYSTEM

Don't trust your memory. Step out of the dark ages, and put a PC to work if you're not already computerized. They've got infallible memories, type perfectly, dial indefatigably. This isn't a computer book, so I won't go into specific A/R software, but be assured that there's plenty available. No matter what business you're in, a PC in A/R will pay for itself quickly.

When the first payment arrives on time, reinforce the behavior you like. The best way is to place a two-minute call and simply say, "Thank you." Next best is to jot a thank-you note. But written notes don't really cost less, and they certainly lose the personal impact.

And if the check doesn't arrive as promised, beware. The

die is cast at the beginning of the repayment period. Don't let that first payment slip. Pull out the stops. Call and say that you'll dispatch a messenger to help the person live up to *his* promise. Stay on top of it.

CAUTION!

Accounts Receivable is one area where you need to consult with legal counsel or your local credit manager's association. State laws vary and are complex and confusing. Be sure you know when you may and may not call consumers at home. Be careful not to exceed the allowed number of contacts, or else you'll be sued for harassment. Certainly avoid anything that may be construed as intimidation. If you tell a debtor that you're turning the matter over to your attorney in forty-eight hours, you must do so, or it's just an empty threat. Believe it or not, you could end up being sued for *not* turning the matter over to your attorney. We live in funny legal times.

9

PROFITABLE TELEMARKETING: MEETING YOUR CUSTOMERS' NEEDS

When your goal is to meet the needs of your marketplace, there's no tool as powerful as the telephone. Businesses in virtually every industry are experiencing huge (and very profitable) successes with telemarketing. The word wasn't even used until late 1967. Today, it's the marketing force that's sweeping the business scene.

In May 1983 *U.S. News and World Report* surveyed the greatest growth career opportunities for the balance of this century. They found that the number one growth area—marketing by telephone—offered more new careers than the next nineteen front-runners combined! Only two other careers nudged past the million mark (computer-aided design engineers, 1,220,000; software writers, 1,080,000); but telemarketing is projected to create *8 million* new careers in the same period.

YOU MEAN PHONE SALES?

No. And yes. Most people confuse telemarketing with the old-fashioned, sometimes high-pressure boiler-room operations in which coffee-guzzling hucksters plague consumers (usually just as they sit down for dinner) with unbelievable offers. We've all had them. I make it a habit to monitor these calls and always say yes (unless they ask for a credit card number) and document what happens. There's always a catch.

"Mr. Walther, I've got some great news for you! Some months back, somebody at your company ordered some stationery items from us and you were automatically entered in our once-a-year appreciation contest. It's our way of showing that we appreciate your business. I'm happy to tell you that yours is the company that won! I've been authorized to award you a four-day, three-night vacation at the fabulous Grand Regency Resort in Las Vegas. Or, you can have a one-week cruise in the Caribbean. Sounds great, doesn't it?"

Of course, I've never purchased anything from the company. They've just pulled my name from the phone book. (What a coincidence, several of my business-owning friends in the same phone book were also grand-prize winners!)

The Grand Regency turns out to be a fourth-rate motel, and the cruise has quite a few strings attached. Ultimately, you discover that you have to sit through a "Time Share Holiday Presentation" (a.k.a. "high-pressure sales pitch for overpriced cubicles at a sleazy converted motel") once you've reached your destination. What few people ever discover is that the companies who make your "valuable grand prize" awards are actually paid by the "resorts" for every body they can pull in.

Whatever connotations old-fashioned telephone selling may have, telemarketing in the business world today connotes a highly professional marketing medium; not a tactical weapon but a strategic tool in profit-minded companies' marketing mixes. It's used in conjunction with direct mail, media advertising, and face-to-face visits. While it does include selling, telemarketing runs the gamut of activities related to serving the marketplace. That means using the phone for:

- market research, to find out what the market wants and what it thinks of what you're already doing,
- inquiry handling, to answer questions and furnish information when potential buyers respond to advertising,
- prospect qualifying, to ensure that only people who do have a serious need get the attention of your sales department,
- appointment scheduling, to allocate costly personal sales meetings only to prospects who do want to meet and will honor their appointments,
- closing sales, often eliminating the need to make in-person visits,
- follow-up reinforcement, to be sure that the customer is pleased with the decisions he has made,
- long-term relationship nurturing, to make certain that you and your customers remain in sync,
- referral prospecting, to find out if your customers have colleagues and friends you should also be serving,
- customer service, to rapidly correct any problems encountered along the way.

The telephone is a vital tool in the entire marketing process, not just selling.

WHY NOW?

The reason most often cited for telemarketing's emergence is the high cost of face-to-face selling. Each year, McGraw-Hill surveys businesses across the country and computes the average cost of a face-to-face sales visit. Today, that figure is well over $200. That takes into account travel expenses, time, auto costs, and so on. The Sales and Marketing Executives Association estimates that, on average, five personal visits are made for every successfully completed sale. It can cost over $1000 to close a sale!

Part of the reason for that high cost is that outside salespeople often earn big bucks, but offer relatively low productivity. The highest estimate of actual selling time I've come across is 39 percent. Travel, waiting, completing paperwork, et cetera chews up at least 61 percent of a salesman's time.

On the other hand, inside salespeople—professional telemarketers—can actually converse with prospects and customers during 75 percent of their "on" time. And the cost per contact is more like $20. So there are compelling cost advantages to selling by phone.

But that's just one viewpoint. What's really more significant is how *buyers* feel about telemarketing. The Arthur Anderson Company accounting firm has researched the important wholesale distribution channel to determine what customers care about in the way vendors service them. The study begins with 1970 and projects ahead to 1990. In 1970, buyers ranked a knowledgeable, attentive outside salesman as their number-one concern. Speed of delivery ranked second, and price third. By 1980, speed of delivery was first, price second, and the outside salesman dropped to third place. In 1985, speed of delivery was still first, but the salesman dropped to fifth place, and a good telemarketing rep scored second. The projection for 1990: Buyers will be *most* interested in good telemarketing reps, speed of delivery will be second, range of products third, price fourth, and the concern for a good outside salesman will drop to eighth!

Telemarketing isn't booming just because it's a cheaper way for companies to sell. It's rapidly growing because buyers want fast, convenient, economical ways to purchase. They don't want salesmen sitting in their lobbies, chatting over lunch, and wasting their time.

It's really no surprise. The whole world, and certainly the pace of business, has gone through time warp in recent decades. When you run out of floppy disks for the office computer, you wouldn't think of writing to a supply company, waiting for a salesman to come by with a sample case, placing your order, waiting for him to return to the warehouse, and then waiting for a delivery truck to bring the box to you. Just a few years ago, that's how we all did business. Now we want to place one call, have a capable, professional, knowledgeable person answer our questions, recommend the product that will meet our need, and send it immediately.

THE PROFESSION IS BORN

Between 1980 and 1985:

- a glossy magazine named *Telemarketing* devoted exclusively to the industry began publication and several others followed,
- the American Telemarketing Association was formed, boasting a national membership of high-level executives,
- the Telemarketing Foundation created a comprehensive curriculum of training programs offered to professionals around the nation,
- several telemarketing trade shows began bringing together hundreds of exhibitors and thousands of managers and communicators, and
- countless newsletters began publishing practical application techniques and news of industry developments.

Telemarketing isn't a few scattered groups of buzzed-out phone salesmen. It's truly the fastest-emerging profession in America.

NAME ANY INDUSTRY

It's hard to think of any industry which isn't using telemarketing already. While there are plenty of firms that sell to consumers at home, the biggest telemarketing growth is in the business-to-business marketplace.

Pharmaceutical companies are sending fewer salesmen off to medical buildings. They find that even male impotence screening devices can be marketed by phone. Although doctors are among the most difficult sales prospects to reach, it's easier to connect by phoning than by camping out in a reception room.

Computer companies market huge amounts of hardware by phone. Office computers have practically become commodity items. IBM has a facility that telemarkets PCs in gross quantities—144 at a crack.

The U.S. Department of Commerce sells historical weather data by phone. I was hired to train a team of government meteorologists holed up in a huge warehouse filled with weather logs dating back to George Washington's daily journal of conditions on the battlefront. Insurance investigators call and ask, "Is there any way I can find out if the streets were slippery when one of our policyholders skidded off the road and hit a cow in Beaumont, Texas, four years ago?"

Sure is. For a price, trained meteorologists will by telephone tell you how hard the wind was blowing in Oshkosh at 11:00 A.M. on October 11, 1911.

Corporate jet manufacturers use telemarketing extensively. Of course, the final sale may not be consummated by phone, but extensive telemarketing screening and qualifying processes weed out all but the most serious, financially able prospects.

One of my clients sells mainframe computer software at $30,000 for a reel of encoded tape. There is no visit. The entire transaction is handled by phone. The multistage sales sequence involves personal calls that begin with the executive secretary, proceed to the president and the VP of finance, and ultimately reach the data processing manager.

Every kind of insurance company markets extensively by phone. My consulting projects have ranged from liability policies for owners of small private planes and helicopters to prearranged funerals and burials for the aging.

A video dating service in California does a huge business telemarketing social arrangements. The prospecting, screening, interviewing, and selling is all done by phone. You pay for a set number of introductions and view videotapes of your potential heartthrobs at home.

If your company isn't already using telemarketing, it certainly will be soon. Your competitors are using it now. This is the fastest-moving marketing revolution in America. Don't let it pass you by.

INBOUND TELEMARKETING

Many companies have handled telephone orders for many years. They've usually approached this as "order entry," a largely clerical function. Customers did get their orders placed more quickly than if they'd mailed them, but got little sense of real contact with a telephone professional.

One of the first evidences of telemarketing's upgraded professionalism is the way inbound calls are handled. Telemarketers are now being taught to realize that their role is not just to record orders, but to meet customers' needs—including those which are unexpressed. There are three stages in meeting the caller's needs: reacting professionally, actively probing to find out the customer's unstated needs, and reaching to discover long-term needs.

REACTING PROFESSIONALLY

The most evident lack of professionalism has been in the failure to use the simple basics of conscious contact. Telemarketers are now trained to be very conscious of the way they answer calls, adjust body postures, vary their voices, use feedback loops, and verify communications.

The result is higher levels of customer satisfaction. Orders are handled with far less likelihood of error, and a much higher level of rapport. One of the conscious aims is to go beyond the accurate recording of facts and build personal bridges. The emotional elements may be even more important than the objective facts exchanged. And inbound calls sometimes involve on-the-spot complaint handling where all the principles explored in "Wired Emotions" come into play.

In short, the first step in handling inbound order calls is to act as a telephone professional rather than an order-taking clerk.

ACTIVELY PROBING

The biggest short-term profits in inbound telemarketing result from meeting customer's unexpressed needs. This is variously known as "upping the order" or "cross-selling," but I think it's much more productive to look at it from the customer's viewpoint. We know that customers are always looking for ways to save money, and time, and generally increase the value they receive from any transaction.

Active probing is simply a matter of looking for ways to meet these common, but unexpressed needs. Telemarketers can always save their customers money by suggesting larger quantities of a regularly-ordered item. Unit prices almost always drop, so you do me a favor when you show me that my cost per item will decrease when I take advantage of the larger order size. The most effective approach is to cite incremental costs. If you call to order 50 vinyl binders from me, the cost will be $2.70 each. But if you order 100, the cost may drop to $2.25. One way to communicate the savings is to say the price drops over 16 percent. But a much stronger approach is to say, "The total cost for fifty binders is $135. But one hundred would cost $225. That means that the extra fifty cost only $90 more. In other words, the additional binders are really costing you only $1.80 each."

If I do have an ongoing need for binders, and I'm willing (as demonstrated by my order for fifty in the first place) to pay $2.70 each for them, wouldn't I be crazy not to buy another fifty at $1.80—a savings of 33 percent? If I knew that I could have saved 33 percent on those binders and you didn't call it to my attention, I'd feel that you were doing me a disservice.

I'm also interested in saving time. If you can save me the trouble of placing another order call a month from now, when I'm out of binders, you're saving me time and trouble, too. You're also minimizing my chances of finding the cupboard bare when I have a pressing need. Suggesting a larger quantity saves me time and money.

I've trained inbound telemarketers in many industries and they always find that customers are grateful to know of these savings *when they're pointed out*. At 20th Century Plastics, a rapidly growing division of Avery International that sells more than $40 million in plastic sheet protectors and related products each year, telemarketers have found that many customers call every couple of weeks to order another 250 sheet protectors. Over the course of the year, they may order six or seven thousand sheet protectors. But they take twenty-five phone calls to do it. The 20th Century telemarketers now routinely suggest "blanket purchase orders" in situations like these. In a single call, the customer can arrange to have 250 sent every two weeks for the next year. Doing so doesn't just save a couple of dozen phone calls, it can save up to 42 percent by getting the price break in effect at six thousand pieces instead of the much higher per-unit price for orders of 250.

The customer comes out way ahead. And so does the company. Actively probing for unexpressed needs is a way to offer much more value. And it's also a way to dramatically boost revenues and profits. Both parties benefit if telemarketers look for ways to help customers and make suggestions to them.

REACHING FOR LONG-TERM NEEDS

The true professionals take a step beyond short-term revenues and satisfy long-term needs. We know that customers are always interested in being better served. They're certainly interested in getting better value and more utility. I always train telemarketers to take this third step when handling inbound calls. They ask for suggestions to improve long-range relationships and product design.

> "Mr. Taub, we're always looking for ways to improve our service. If there were one or two things we could do that would make it easier for you to do business with us, I'd appreciate your telling me."

"John, you've been ordering lots of these video cassette storage boxes, so you're really an expert on how well they work. If you could make a single change or improvement to them, what would you do?"

Questions like these look out for your long-term interests, and they certainly help your customers, too.

Training telemarketers to be professional in their handling of inbound calls yields big profits and higher customer satisfaction. Successful telemarketing puts everybody ahead.

OUTBOUND TELEMARKETING

Phone sales used to be thought of as those guys who'd call, rudely brush past your secretarial screen with less than honest tactics, and talk your ear off. Today's telemarketing professionals view themselves as partners in problem solving. As long as they stay focused on the needs of their customers, rather than simply their own needs, long-term, mutually rewarding relationships are the result.

THE   CPR METHOD

I advise telemarketers to breathe life into customer relationships by practicing CPR. It's the simple foundation on which all buying relationships are built. Notice that I say "buying" rather than "selling." Successful outbound telemarketers are those whose customers want to buy from them, not those who force a sale. The method works like this:

C: Consult   The starting point is to ask questions. One of my telemarketing projects involved an outbound program marketing "Custom Calling Features" for customers of New York Telephone. They were offering Call Forwarding, Call Waiting, and Speed Dialing features to subscribers in exchange areas that had been converted to electronic switching equipment. The telemarketers weren't having such good luck when they called residents and attempted to explain the features. For example, they'd call someone in a suburban area and essentially say,

> "We're offering subscribers in your area Call Waiting and Call Forwarding. This means that if you're on the phone and someone else tries to reach you, you hear a tone in your ear and you can switch to the second call. Call Forwarding means that you can designate a number anywhere in the world where you'd like your calls forwarded, and they'll automatically be switched to that number. Would you like to sign up?"

Would *you*? Who cares to have a tone in his ear? And very few people are interested in being able to shunt their calls to someone else's phone. The telemarketers were talking about features. Nobody's interested in features. We're all selfishly interested in ourselves. We care about benefits.

The starting point in restructuring New York Tel's outbound program was coming up with questions that would help reveal customers' needs that the features would satisfy.

> "Mr. Schweizer, when people say they have a hard time reaching you, do they usually say your line's often busy, or that you're never around to answer the phone? When you're away for the weekend, or working long hours, are you more concerned about the danger of burglaries at your home, or are you more concerned about missing important calls?"

The starting point in effective outbound telemarketing is to find out about your prospect's needs—not what you have to offer but what your customer needs. If Mr. Schweizer says that people can't ever reach him because he's always on the phone, and that rising crime in his neighborhood is a concern, we know something about what his needs are and what benefits may appeal to him.

P: Personalize   The next step, after *consulting* with the customer to find out what his needs are, is to *personalize* the benefits you offer to the needs he has expressed.

"Mr. Hopkins, I know what you mean about crime being a concern. My neighborhood's been getting worse, too. One benefit of the call-forwarding feature is that you can always answer your home phone, even when you're not there. Burglars usually call before they break in. When there's no answer, they know the coast is clear. Some of my customers go into the office on weekends and have their calls forwarded there. That way, even if someone suspects you're not at home, they hear your voice when they call to check and you've prevented a problem.

"You also mentioned that people have trouble reaching you because you use the phone a lot. The thing heavy phone users like you most appreciate about call waiting is that people can always reach them, even while they're talking to somebody else. Rather than reaching a busy signal, they reach you. You can switch back and forth between the two calls easily and either take a message, or call one party back later. It's very convenient."

R: Recommend   The key to succeeding in telemarketing is meeting needs. *Consulting* lets you find out what they are. *Personalizing* lets you show the prospect how he will personally benefit by having his needs met. Rather than forcing a sale, truly effective telemarketers make sure they're in a position to *ecommend* that prospects take advantage of solutions to their needs.

"Mr. Schweizer, based on what you've told me about your concerns for security and the problem of people not being able to get through on your line, I *recommend* that you take advantage of both of these new services. I can save you fifteen percent on the monthly charges by ordering both at once. Of course, the call forwarding will also help you cut down on missed calls when you're working late, or visiting friends. Would you like me to expedite these services for you, or just have them added at the start of next month?"

Inbound or outbound, professional telemarketers adopt the goal of meeting as many customer needs as possible. Doing so creates short-term and long-term customer satisfaction—and profits.

SUCCESS IS THE COMMON THEME

Corporate boardrooms and professional conferences have a common theme these days. There's always talk of a successful telemarketing program. Sales costs are often slashed by as much as 75 percent. And closing ratios are frequently higher for phone calls than for personal visits.

According to John Ruth, vice president of sales at Massey-Ferguson,". . . our telemarketing program, in concert with other marketing initiatives, was the single most significant factor in taking Massey-Ferguson from reported losses totaling over $900 million in the last four years, to three consecutive profitable quarters in 1984. . . ."

Countless other success stories are being created right now. The numbers will swell. Using *Phone Power* will ensure that the profession grows with a reputation for intergrity as well as profits.

EPILOGUE

The typical business phoning scenarios related in *Phone Power*'s introduction are all too common. You've been trapped in them many times. The tangled bureaucracies that transfer you endlessly, the frustrating games of phone tag, the emotionally charged calls that get out of hand, and the ineffective departments in your own organization that go through the motions but don't achieve their objectives.

Although these enervating, time-robbing, unproductive exchanges are commonplace, they're totally preventable. You can change them all. If you reread those introductory examples now, you'll immediately identify what went wrong and how they can be turned around.

But the telephone techniques in *Phone Power* aren't hypothetical. Whatever you aim to accomplish when using the phone, treat it as an opportunity for goal phoning and put the principles of conscious contact to work.

The very next time you dial or your phone rings, treat that instrument as your ally. The telephone is your most profitable business tool.

AN INVITATION FROM THE AUTHOR

I'd love to hear about *your* Phone Power. If your organization is doing something unusual, or if you practice a special phone technique, please tell me about it.

If you want full-size prototypes of the Message Slip, Call Planning and Objectives form, and the Complaint Handling Guide, please send me a self-addressed, stamped envelope. I'll be glad to send you master copies with my compliments.

If you are planning a meeting or convention and need a speaker who will motivate your people to perform more effectively and efficiently, please call me at (213) 821-4100. Thank you.

George Walther
The TelExcel® Companies
Divisions of George R. Walther, Inc.
3004 Pacific Avenue
Marina del Rey, CA 90291

BIBLIOGRAPHY

Bandler, Richard, and Grinder, John. *Frogs into Princes*. Moab, Utah: Real People Press, 1979.

Blanchard, Dr. Kenneth. *The One-Minute Manager*. New York: William Morrow, 1982.

Cooper, Morton. *Change Your Voice, Change Your Life*. New York: Mac-Millan, 1984.

Fisher, Roger, and Ury, William. *Getting to Yes*. Boston: Houghton Mifflin Company, 1981.

LeBoeuf, Michael. *The Greatest Management Principle in the World*. New York: G. P. Putnam's Sons, 1985.

McCormack, Mark. *What They Don't Teach You at Harvard Business School*. New York: Bantam Books, 1984.

Naisbitt, John. *Megatrends*. New York: Warner Books, 1982.

Peters, Thomas J., and Waterman, Robert H. *In Search of Excellence*. New York: Harper & Row, 1982.

INDEX